Russian Bride Guide

Russian Bride Guide

How to Meet, Court and Marry a Woman from the Former Soviet Union

Stuart J. Smith

with

Olga Maslova

First published in Great Britain by Scruton Publishing Co., 2008

Copyright © Stuart J. Smith 2006-2008

This book is copyright under the Berne Convention.

No reproduction without permission.

All rights reserved.

The right of Stuart J. Smith to be identified as author of this work has been asserted by him in accordance with sections 77 and 78 of the Copyright, Designs and Patents Act, 1988.

A CIP catalogue record for this book is available from the British Library

ISBN 978-0-9556874-0-2

Printed and bound in Great Britain

DISCLAIMER

The authors intend that this book be relied on purely as a helpful stepping stone on the path to education on the subject matter. Neither the authors nor the publisher accept any legal responsibility for the adequacy, accuracy, completeness or reasonableness of any of the information, statements, opinions or comments referred to or contained within this book nor for any damage or loss, howsoever caused directly or indirectly occasioned by any such reliance. The opinions expressed are the authors' own and any examples contained within this book are for illustrative purposes only.

About the Authors

Stuart J. Smith and Olga Maslova are a married English/Russian couple who have been through the whole experience personally from start to finish and who live part time in the former Soviet Union. Stuart has been visiting the former Soviet Union regularly for over a decade. He is now an administrator and an advisor on one of the largest, most-respected internet advice forums on this subject.

Olga is a multi-lingual Russian woman with two degrees in psychology and personal experience running a small introduction agency herself. Before marrying, she was a psychology lecturer at a university in Samara, Russia. She has extensive experience both helping women from Russia, Ukraine and Belarus seeking foreign men, and working with men from the US, Canada, Australia, New Zealand and Europe seeking an FSU wife. The joint experience contained in this book is unrivalled.

***

Посвящается моей прекрасной жене Ольге, без участия, поддержки и терпения которой создание этой книги было бы невозможным.

Contents

Introduction 1

Chapter One: An Overview of the Process 4

Chapter Two: Introspection 9

Chapter Three: How Much Will This Cost Me? 20

Chapter Four: Age Differences and What Russian Women Want 29

Chapter Five: Scams, Scammers and Sharp Practice 50

Chapter Six: How to Select an Agency or Contact Method 67

Chapter Seven: Choosing Women to Contact 80

Chapter Eight: Making Progress - Communication 91

Chapter Nine: Overcoming Language Barriers 107

Chapter Ten: Your First Meeting 117

Chapter Eleven: Visiting Russia 134

Chapter Twelve: Maintaining Long-Distance Relationships 153

Chapter Thirteen: Visas 160

Chapter Fourteen: After Her Arrival — Helping Her Adapt and Creating a Family 173

Chapter Fifteen: Other Resources 194

Introduction

When I was a small child, I was mystified by the secret country that Russia used to be. I remember my Grandmother telling me of my Great Grandfather's fluent knowledge of the Russian language and of his travels to Russia in the 1930's. In her bookcase were some very old Russian language books that belonged to my Great Grandfather. As a child, I would look at the strange Cyrillic characters in them and I would wonder how anyone could possibly understand them. Later, as a teenager, I would watch President Gorbachev, President Reagan and Prime Minister Thatcher on the news. My wonderment continued as I contemplated the former Soviet Union. Since then, of course, it has become the Russian Federation, the Commonwealth of Independent States and the EU Baltic States.

Elton Johns' lyrics, "…you'll never know anything about my home…," rang through my head when I was in my teens. It was many years before I realised that Nikita is, in fact, a man's name in Russia. (In any case, Elton's song was about an East German girl.) My thoughts have often turned to Russia, over the years, as I considered the mysterious territory, which, as the USSR, was a sixth of the world's land mass. After Perestroika, Russia began to open up to the West. Occasionally, I would see enchanting Slavic Russian women on the television as well as many now-famous sports stars.

As the internet spread across the world, Russian women became big news and big business, especially for the new internet dating agencies. Unfortunately, as you will learn in this book, dating agencies can sometimes be a very dirty business. My first foray into the former Soviet Union was a trip to Estonia in 1998. Having received their independence from Russia in 1991 and prior to joining the EU, they were still in the midst of their transformation to capitalism. I was very intrigued with this country, which still bore the *Hammer and Sickle* motif on their buildings, as well as the Russian signs and language. I was even more intrigued by the women; I visited again the following week.

I have been to Estonia many times, since then, and have even driven a few times, passing through Poland, Lithuania and Latvia in the process. Naturally, I encountered quite a few women in the course of my travels, both by design as well as by accident. Suffice to say, it was the beginning of a long, steep learning curve.

Following the demise of a long-term relationship with a local woman, I decided to investigate the subject of Russian women further. Since I had always been so fascinated by Russia, the Motherland was the obvious place for me to go. I wanted to see these mythical women in their natural habitat and their spiritual homeland.

When I first began to scratch the surface of this topic, I learned that propaganda, internet fraud, cons and scams were plentiful. I slowly learned about the mentality and the motivations of typical Russian women and, more importantly, that the crazy notion of finding a Russian wife may actually be workable.

The most important part of this endeavor is to learn what one should and should not do. If one goes it alone, it could take a few marriages and fifteen years of your life to learn the pitfalls. By then, you would have

Introduction

poured thousands into the pockets of agencies with negligible progress to show for your efforts.

My personal journey resulted in my 2006 marriage to my lovely Russian wife, Olga, the co-author of this book. Our personal experiences, as well as the experience of guiding others, are what prompted us to write this book. In addition to my normal work, I am an administrator of a comprehensive, internet-based advice forum, dealing with relationships with Russian women.

My wife owns and operates a small agency website, which provides introductions, scrupulously accurate translations, three-way telephone services and visa support. The words which you are about to read are the culmination of a decade of my experience and a lifetime of my wife's experience. I very much hope that you will enjoy the reading and that you will benefit from knowledge, which could otherwise take many years to acquire.

Chapter One
An Overview of the Process

So you want a Russian wife. Is it possible? Some elements of the media would have you believe that Russian women are all passport-seeking harlots who will bleed you financially dry and then run back to Russia at the drop of a hat. You are here to learn both the good and the bad.

Yes, the media negative does exist and there has even been the occasional press report of a Russian woman killing her shiny new husband. However, you are here to find out about the possibilities for the informed man, aren't you? So, to return to the question of if it is possible, the simple answer is yes. You too can find a lovely wife in Russia or in one of the former Soviet Union countries and she may even exceed all of your expectations. But what you are here to learn is that, when you delve into the very dirty barrel that is the Russian international dating scene, usually conducted via the internet, you have to look long and hard, with expert knowledge, to find your pearl amongst the dross. There are many pitfalls that can leave you financially drained as well as emotionally scarred.

There are opinions touted by the ill-informed about Western men pursuing Russian women as future brides and companions. There is both truth in the reports of scam victims and also in the fairytale endings posted on various internet dating sites and forums. I *do* believe, and indeed am living proof, that it is possible to find, via the internet, a beautiful, sincere, charming and loving lady from Russia to love, who will love you, and with whom you can build a stable family. However, what it takes

An Overview of the Process

to do so is accurate, up-to-date information to help you to complete the process. You will need to learn the best way to meet her, how to determine which women are genuine and how to smooth the complex pathway to developing a lasting and loving relationship with a former Soviet Union lady.

Mail-order bride is a popular term that is often used by the media and many dating websites. It is a term that conjures up an image of surfing a website, clicking on a model-like picture of a Russian girl, sending a few e-mails and, in a few months, you will have a supermodel in your kitchen and in your bedroom. Does that sound like fun? Yes, of course it does; most fantasies do! The term *mail-order bride* is probably one of the most inaccurate media-concocted descriptions of the women in this process that anyone could imagine, but it is one of the most widely used. That is one of the many reasons why most men misunderstand this process significantly and a reason that thousands of men have spent a lot of money on this endeavor and have gotten nowhere.

In order to demonstrate the unfair application of the term *mail-order bride*, consider that a relationship between an Englishman and a German woman is said to be an international relationship, yet a relationship between an Englishman and a Russian woman is likely to get her labeled as a mail-order bride. With the German woman, people simply say, "Oh, his wife is German." In the case of the Russian woman, they are more likely to say, "He married one of those Russian mail-order brides, you know." The media and, by extension, the public, love to label people in this way.

The cover of this book depicts a passport-clutching Russian woman climbing from her packaging box; it is deliberate parody to ridicule the mail-order bride label. It was chosen to play on your probable indoctrination by the media and to make you pick the book up. You did, didn't you? Most agency websites use the term *mail-order bride* in their marketing, not because it is accurate, but because it is the term that people recognize.

Introspection is the first task. You will examine your expectations and you will consider your reasons for seeking a Russian bride. I will attempt to demystify the media and agency hype and show you what you can really expect. I will explain to you a little about the real Russia I have experienced and where my wife has lived for approximately thirty years. I will explain the mentality of the women you will encounter. You will learn how to be certain that they are indeed women with whom you are communicating. An apparently sexy internet Svetlana may actually be *Hairy Boris* or *Fat Yuri* in disguise!

I seek to lay bare the dubious practices of some agencies that disregard your feelings and only want your money. This book will educate you as to where and how to start and why you don't just open up *Google* and type "Russian women" with your credit card in hand; unless you really know what you are doing, and even then, I don't advise you do that!

You will learn the difference between methods of contact and the difference between types of agencies and websites. We will discuss communicating by e-mail, telephone, snail mail, web-based media and SMS text message. You will learn how to compose your initial introduction letter and what type of photographs to send. We all know first impressions count in any sphere of life, more so I believe on this topic. You will learn how to overcome language barriers and difficulties, fish out the frauds, the do's and the don'ts (which are important as these women are easily

An Overview of the Process

offended), how to make yourself shine ahead of other men who may be contacting the woman.

You will learn about Russian customs, traditions and superstitions, not to mention common sense on the age-old debate about age differences and what is reasonable, sensible and attainable in that regard. I will discuss travel to Russia and to the former Soviet Union (FSU) and I will discuss the differences between Russia itself and the surrounding FSU countries. You will read travel tips, visa tips and information about bringing your chosen woman back to your country.

You will be encouraged to consider what actually happens when she gets to your country, the psychological and adaptation issues that will arise, how to assist her in what will be the biggest thing that she will ever do in her entire life and how you can both handle it together as a cohesive team.

It is my aim, with this book, to assist the serious man who is considering a Russian wife how to save a lot of money as well as emotional heartache and how to do it correctly the first time. I offer practical advice based on personal experience of my wife and me. I attempt to offer an insight into the average Russian woman's psyche. This has been corrected and added to along the way, not only by my wife Olga, but also by other Russian women we know and have met.

I refer interchangeably throughout this book to Russian women and FSU women. Those terms herein include women from the Former Soviet Union (FSU) and includes the following countries: Belarus, Estonia, Lithuania, Russia, Armenia, Georgia, Latvia, Moldova and Ukraine.

Azerbaijan, Kazakhstan, Uzbekistan, Tajikistan, Turkmenistan and

Kyrgyzstan are technically included by default in the abbreviation *FSU*, but for our purposes, usually lesser so. My definition also includes the territories under Russian control and/or within the Russian Federation such as Kaliningrad together with all the small republics within Russia such as Chuvashia and Tatarstan (indeed the reason why Russia is a federation). The whole area is referred to as the FSU (Former Soviet Union) and I use Russia and the FSU interchangeably in this book. Monetary values used in this book are quoted in US Dollars, as that is a currency most people around the world can think in.

Finding a Russian wife is not an easy process. Getting her home can also be fraught with stress (more so if you are American). You will encounter disappointment, frustration and most certainly significant expense. But is it worth it? Many men who are happily married to Russian women and who are smiling like Cheshire cats think so. I am one of them. I want you to be one of those guys also.

My aim, with this book, is to make you go into this life-changing endeavor fully informed and with your eyes wide open, knowing exactly what to expect. I want to enable you to unlock the mystery that is the much-fabled FSU lady. I am not going to sugarcoat it for you, so you may not like it or you may not expect some of it. I hope that you enjoy reading this book as much as we have enjoyed writing it, and I hope you can take something from it to help with your own personal success with a Russian woman. So let's get to the bones of the issue and continue.

Chapter Two
Introspection

So you are browsing the internet personal ads and dating agencies considering a Russian woman, then? I hope so, or else you have bought the wrong book!

This is the chapter where you abandon all of your pre-conceived ideas about Russian women at the door, forget most of what you have read on agency websites and, especially, most of what you have read and seen in your local media. The media often report biased information about Russia, and especially about Russian women. This is usually biased, based on the current political motivations in the country of publishing. You are here to learn about the real situation: How to get a Russian wife, what she is all about and, more importantly, how to keep her!

So why do you want a Russian woman? Many men are chasing a traditional 1950's June Cleaver fantasy, convinced that they will be able to marry the dream that is a slim, stocking-clad domestic goddess in four-inch heels by day and a salivating nymphomaniac by night. Some elements of that are just about possible because some Russian women have traits that do cater to those desires. Depending on your experience with your local women, a typical Russian woman may indeed be a breath of fresh air for you.

The thing to remember is that women are women wherever they may hail from. Of course, upbringing and culture plays a major part in a person, but the concept touted by some that Russian women adore housework and cooking to a degree that you will be swept back in time to the 1950s is as improbable with a Russian woman as it is with a woman from your country.

If you type "Russian woman," "mail-order bride" or "foreign bride" into an internet search engine, you will get many thousands of results. It is very tempting to browse through the photographs of scantily clad women. You may even convince yourself that these girls are all itching for a better life outside of Russia, that you can pretty much pick any one you choose off the shelf and that you can give her a better life in the West. On that point, you would be wrong, those days are long gone, but we will go into that later.

However, what we must look at first is why you are seriously considering this venture in the first place. Are you old, fat, ugly and bald? Can't you get a woman at home? Do not be angry at me for asking because many people will ask you similar questions in the future; you had better grow a thick skin now. You may be old, fat, ugly and bald; you may also be a young, muscle-bound stud with a full head of hair, teeth like an American toothpaste commercial and a triangular torso. Despite the public perception, there is no particular type of man that seriously considers a Russian woman. This endeavor may be for you.

When you ask a group of ill-advised men who are thinking about a Russian woman why they are thinking about it, sometimes you get these kinds of replies:

- "Have you seen those photographs? I want to get me one of those!"
- "I wanted to trade my ex-wife in for a younger model!"

Introspection

- "Russian women like housework, don't they?"
- "Imagine that sexy accent in bed!"
- "Russian women like cooking, right?"
- "It's easy to do; they all want a passport, correct?"
- "If it does not work out, I can send her back to Russia and get another."
- "They prefer much older men, don't they?"

If your thoughts are similar to the ones above, then I am sorry to burst your bubble, but Russia is not the place you should look for a wife just yet, at least not until you have finished this book. You have been deceived by dating websites, media hype and possibly your friends in the pub. You should realize that the closest that most of your friends have been to a Russian woman is watching Anna Kournikova on TV. But, since you are not Russian either and you are unaware of the socio-economic and cultural conditions of Russia, it would be beneficial for us to start from scratch. We will examine the quotations above later. For now, we will continue with examining you!

Western men, such as me, who are married to Russian women, quote many reasons for their initial search for a Russian woman, the most popular of which are:

- They wanted a slim, sexy, educated woman and such women are in short supply at home.
- They wanted a wife whose first priority was her children and husband, not her career. (I am referring to traditional family values.)
- They say that the intelligent, attractive local women were either

married already or divorced with four kids and are psychologically damaged.

- They all speak of some degree of disillusionment, after many relationships with their local women.
- There are very few nice women in their small town.
- They perceive many of their local women to be bra-burning feminists who are humorless and too politically correct.
- They simply don't find fat, lazy, smoking, junk food-eating, sloppy, flip flop-wearing women to be attractive. Unfortunately, this is all that they seem to see at home.

If the reasons above sound familiar to you then you have arrived at the front door to this endeavor for similar reasons to those who have gone before you. Once you lose the mindset that you are dealing with a purchasable commodity, then you are moving towards the correct frame of mind for your forthcoming adventure.

I have identified five basic types of men who look to Russia for a bride. If you can identify yourself and give some deep thought to your motivations, it will serve you well when you read the rest of this book and in your forthcoming adventure. The five groups are as follows:

Group one: All-round confident type of coves who enjoy decent success with their local women. Going to Russia for these guys is a conscious choice, executed merely to add another string to their bow, to widen their dating pool or to search for traits in women that they *perceive* that they can't find at home.

Group two: Guys who seek something (usually an enormous age gap) that they don't have a snowball's chance in hell of getting at home. These would be the *maximum economic exploitation* guys and the sex tourists.

Group three: Guys who live in remote places where women are few in number. This would not be a problem in the UK as we are small and densely packed; I am thinking of rural parts of the US, Canada and Australia here really.

Group four: Guys that have, for whatever reason, relocated, settled and partially integrated in Russia (probably because of work). This would be the most natural basis for a relationship, of course, as it replicates the domestic dating scene, especially if they know the Russian language.

Group five: Guys who have no choice but to seek abroad as they are rejected by their peers either due to their physical traits, lack of confidence, people skills or other reasons. The *can't get laid in a whorehouse* bunch. They see abroad as a get-out-of-jail-free card, hoping that the language barrier will mask their confidence and other issues and they are bolstered by confidence-inspiring media and agency hype, believing foreign women may overlook their less than stellar features and traits.

Of course, most men see themselves as group one, while perceiving other men seeking the same as them as group five. Most of the successfully married guys are from group one, three and four. Groups two and five are grey areas. If you inhabit one of these latter groups you need to read this book several times as you are potentially walking on thin ice; success is possible only for the very well-informed man here. In reality, most of us cross inhabit two or more groups.

During my research for this part of the book, our own experience was not enough. I had to get the opinions of many guys who were already in the chase, and try to deconstruct their replies somewhat to get to the facts. A curious aspect that came up many times was the issue of baggage, both emotional and financial, some of which can presumably be left behind in Russia with a Russian woman. Additionally, with local women, no one wants to buy into substantial credit card debt, car payments, loans, etc., which could easily exceed the total cost of the pursuit in the FSU. Another headache than can be avoided are the issues pertaining to shared parenting of offspring from prior encounters or marriages.

One engaged American man I spoke to summed it up quite well and echoed the thoughts of many others when he said, "There wasn't a snowball's chance in hell of my finding a reasonable solution here that came with her own teeth and without the need to shed fifty pounds, let alone having a passable intellect. The *taking care of their looks* trait is certainly highly desirable and rarely found here, especially after age thirty-five or forty."

When you browse the dating sites you will at first feel like a child in a sweet shop; all of this candy and which one should I choose? The appeal of Russian women is often attributed to their physical beauty. It is pointless to debate about Slavic women's pulchritude; we will discuss the process of choosing one of these beauties in a later chapter.

You must always keep in mind that you are dealing with real people, with real feelings, hopes and aspirations, irrespective of how sexy they may look. If you marry a Russian woman you will not only be changing both of your own lives, but the wider implications will affect all of her

Introspection

family and any children that either of you already have. *Sending her back* will not really be an option. She is not a new sofa; she is a woman who deserves to be treated with respect.

A fact, often overlooked by men entering this endeavor, is that marriage is obligatory if you want a Russian woman. This is almost the only way that she will be able to get a permanent residence visa to your country. You should abandon all ideas of live-in girlfriends, unless you want to live in Russia, as well as any other method that you may have heard of.

Additionally, if a woman is going to change continents to live with you, she wants some security and a modicum of a guarantee that you will not dump her at the drop of a hat. She can find a live-in boyfriend in Russia. She wants the real deal - a devoted husband and a stable family.

Another fact, which is often amazingly overlooked by men entering this endeavor, is that they are going to need to travel a long way and probably quite a few times with no guarantees. Abandon all ideas about your dream woman landing at your local airport for a first meeting after a few e-mails; it is not going to happen! You will be getting on an airplane and flying to the FSU.

Much later, if and when you are successful, you and your woman will apply for a visitor or fiancée visa for her to come to your country. For this, proof that you have met previously, outside of your country, is usually needed before the idea of a visa will even be considered by the authorities. It is best to meet her in her own country so that you can meet her family and friends. So get used to the idea now that there are no shortcuts here. You *are* going to the FSU, probably in the next few months, if you get your act together.

There is a tendency for Westerners to group foreign wives all in one pot. When a man considers a foreign wife, he sometimes considers the former Soviet Union as one option amongst many. Men often think about South American countries such as Venezuela and Brazil, Asian countries such as the Philippines and Thailand and then the FSU. Do not fall into this trap and think that there is little difference. In the FSU you will not be buying the family a goat nor will you be waiting for her to get back from the local go-go bar where she is a dancer before you can call her. (Well, we hope not!)

In the FSU you will mostly be meeting women who are educated to university standard and from an entirely different society than what Asia and Latin America are. Russian women are not peasant girls without education or opportunity in life, nor are Western husbands seen as the big prize that they once were (and still are elsewhere). The days of desperate women seeking only an escape from the FSU are dwindling exceedingly fast as the FSU catches up with, and sometimes exceeds the West in prosperity and opportunity. If you want a bargain basement, mute, lap-dog of a wife, the FSU is not the place to look. Russian women are strong in character and are often more challenging in many respects than Western women are. The FSU is much different from other wife-hunting spots.

Make no mistake about it; Russian women are not a get-out-of-jail-free card for the socially inept and the inexperienced. A man should have comprehensive experience of life and, most especially, of women before he ventures east. A friend of mine, who is married to a Russian woman also, is fond of telling newbie's in this endeavor that, "If you can't do it here, you can't do it there." To an extent, that is true. Too many men hope to find a teenage beauty queen with the best body that they have ever seen, four degrees, fluency in six languages, who has dreamed all her life of finding a middle aged, balding, pot-bellied man of average means in order to treat him like a god and cater to his every whim in his retirement. Unfortunately, if you are an average guy over thirty-five, seeking a good wife and a genuine relationship, you should forget the nineteen-year-old über babes who adorn the homepages of most websites. The real treasure that is true wife material lies elsewhere.

Many men who are drawn to consider foreign ladies, especially Russian ones, are divorced. They have lived in a typically dysfunctional marriage for two or three decades, raised their children and accumulated modest means, during which time they have buried their own personal issues and baggage deep in their psyche. Then, after the kids have left home, either the wife leaves them or they leave the wife.

These guys are suddenly back in the dating game, without modern dating or romance skills, totally clueless about the psychology of single females, especially Russian ones. Such men will often have time and money on their hands and become perfect targets for a certain breed of calculating beautiful Russian woman one can easily encounter. These vulnerable, lonely, clueless guys often run right into these women's arms and foolishly shower them with money and gifts. If you potentially recognize yourself in part of that description, you will avoid this trap when you are in possession of all the facts that you will read in this book.

Many men who lack social skills, particularly men who feel uncomfortable interacting with women and who lack any measurable success with their local women, are drawn into this endeavor, often hoping the language barrier will disguise their negative traits. Yes, these men can easily find a wife in the FSU, but these men are the most susceptible to fraud, bad intent and early divorce, as well. Extreme care must be taken by such men. If this is you, then you should prepare more at home first, socialize more, maybe join some classes and develop your social skills and work on your people skills to make yourself more desirable to women as I will detail later. Such men should possibly consider a full-service agency. We will discuss those types of agencies further.

However, having said all of this, it is perfectly reasonable to expect that, irrespective of what you see in the mirror, you will be able to find and to meet a woman who will be younger than you (by how much you will find out) and who is attractive, certainly at the upper levels of attractiveness of a woman you could expect to date at home and perhaps a good few notches beyond.

Let's be honest here; nobody considers looking abroad to marry an ugly woman and few would want to marry a very dim woman either. Many men will accept beauty over intelligence, some prefer intelligence over beauty. You must decide where you stand. Do not think I am encouraging you not to set your sights high. You must set them very high, but you must remain realistic and accept your own limitations if you want a lovely wife to grow old with. There is no such thing as the perfect woman as the divorced amongst you will know. Perfection is illusory.

For the brave man, seeking no less than a very young super-model standard wife, yes, anything and everything is possible in the FSU. If this is you, you must accept right at the outset that the risks are high, that it may not last and that it may be very expensive in the long run. Extremely large age gaps and wide chasms of incompatibility make for an unstable marriage. Long-term success rates for these marriages are very low indeed. I know of only maybe two that have passed the five-year mark.

Hopefully by now you have grounded yourself a little and torn yourself away from those photographs of nineteen-year-old, silicone-enhanced agency über babes who purport to be fashion models. You should be developing a feeling of what is possible and what is not. You should also now know if I have just shattered your illusions or if what you read above sounded like common sense.

If you still think that you want a Russian wife, then read on.

Chapter Three
How Much Will This Cost Me?

The next issue that you must consider is money. Make no mistake, this will cost you a lot of money, which is another reason you must get it right and which is why you are reading this book. Fear not, you will not be supplying her relatives with a new Lada every year or anything else silly that you may have read. You must, however, factor in expenses to purchase multiple contact details, translation, interpreters, multiple flights, visas, international telephone calls, more flights and just when you think you have it all done then you are buying a rock for her finger, planning a wedding, maybe with foreign guests that you are paying for the travel of.

But, before all of that, your home government will want their pound of flesh for her visas. When you have finished with that, they will want yet more for her driver's license and a whole myriad of other things. Don't forget about extra insurances, medical and dental bills. Is that all? Maybe English lessons, further education and a car? Next she will want to remodel your house and remove any trace of any previous women's taste and your appalling bachelor taste also. Oh and she probably needs a wardrobe upgrade. So do you, for that matter!

Every situation is different, and people differ, of course. I have seen it cost anywhere between $10,000 and $140,000 from joining an agency through to having been together in your country six months down the line after marriage. Yes, of course, you don't need to find this money all at once and some of the costs can be mitigated to a large extent by dating women who already have a reasonable understanding of English and who are sufficiently cultured, widely traveled and mature enough to make the adjustment to a new country and to a new way of life without too much difficulty. Such women are not that hard to find. One must simply have a clear and precise set of goals in mind.

I have seen economical men use free contact agencies, take freight flights, cut corners, scrimp and scrape and still come out smiling. However, is it all worth it? Damn right it is; get it right and you will never look back. It will be the best money you ever spent in your life!

As you might have worked out by now, simply being able to manage a relationship that involves changing continents is not for paupers. You are self-selected to be, from the perspective of the women themselves, quite wealthy. You might think you are middle class and of ordinary means, but, to her, you are not. You are *the wealthy foreign man*; you are seeking a traditional girl from a poorer country.

Why pick girls from poorer countries? Less money means fewer cars and more walking, more walking means slimmer bodies. The same scarcity of money means junk food is unpopular, hence less junk food consumption and thinner bodies again. Thinner bodies are an increasingly much sought after rarity in the West, and anything that is much sought after in the West costs money one way or another.

So let's break it down a bit. Meet our hypothetical man; let's call him Joe from Texas. He starts with an average agency or three, purchases contact information for twenty-five women in total, writes a translated introduction letter to all of them. He is rejected or ignored by ten, enters into correspondence with fifteen of them and in a short while he may have narrowed those down to five good prospects. By that time, he may have sent and received one hundred translated letters in just a few weeks while he weeds out the obvious undesirables. The cost of translation varies from agency to agency. For the sake of argument, let's say that he has paid $10 a letter; he is already at $1000. Plus the price of the original twenty-five contacts that may have cost him a further $30 each, so he has already spent $1750. From his correspondents, one woman shines out from the rest - we shall call her Tatiana.

Having read this book from cover to cover, our Joe then, quite rightly, wants to quickly move on to telephone calls. So, as Sexy Tatiana's English is not too hot, he arranges a three-way translated call for one hour, which costs him $40. He figures that he can manage a few calls without an interpreter also, so he finds a long distance calling deal that allows him to call Ukraine, where Tatiana lives, for 30¢ a minute. Over the next two months Joe spends thirty minutes a day on the phone to Tatiana interspersed with a translated three-way call every week. In two months Joe has spent almost $700 on telephone charges.

By now Joe is ready for a visit. He books his flight out to meet Tatiana for a week, his flights cost him $1800 from Texas to Kiev in Ukraine. Before this he sent Tatiana a gift of a nice English/Russian dictionary and phrasebook and included a few photographs and a letter and a few small items inside. Not trusting the mail service in Ukraine, he used FedEx to send his package. That cost him another $100. Being the nice chap that he is, he found a company on the internet to send Tatiana some flowers a week before he arrived; that cost him another $150.

The expenses outlined above are unremarkable and quite typical of

How Much Will This Cost Me?

pre-meeting expenses for an average American visiting Ukraine. Please bear in mind that Joe has spent $4500 already and he has not yet had a face-to-face meeting with Tatiana. An Englishman or mainland European will have access to cheaper flights; sometimes UK budget airlines serve Ukraine for peanuts. However, the same English man may have met a woman in Novosibirsk in Siberia instead where no budget carriers serve. The resultant connection through Moscow and the added expense of a Russian visa (not needed for Ukraine) may bring the European not far short of what the American spent.

So our Joe is now on the ground in Kiev, Ukraine. He rents an apartment for the week that Tatiana found for him; that costs him $500. A couple of small tasteful gifts that he brought added to his expenses. Restaurants, the occasional interpreter, taxis, etc., add to the tally. His week in Kiev could cost Joe $2000 in total.

Unfortunately, Tatiana and Joe didn't have enough chemistry to incline them to pursue the relationship further. So, after a reasonably fun week, Joe returned home to Texas and hoped to pick up with another of his four remaining favorites. His experience to date has cost Joe $6500 and he is not much further on than when he started, apart from having acquired some very costly experience. Thus far, he has only a failed meeting and a selection of pen friends to show for it.

Joe made a second trip to meet a woman in Russia. Unfortunately, she turned out to be a professional dater who had misrepresented herself somewhat. Consequently, that meeting was unproductive despite costing a further $5000. Joe returned home again, determined to make another attempt with one of the remaining girls on his shortlist.

Joe's next trip took him this time to Belarus to meet Svetlana, with whom he thought that there may be some potential. He had done the telephone get-to-know-you process again and this was his third trip to the FSU. After that more successful week his total bride hunt expenses are approaching $17,000. Joe, of course, wants to make progress with this lady. Therefore, before he leaves, he invests $600 to fund some English lessons and a home internet connection for her in order that she can install Skype to make future communication seamless and more economical, while improving his new lady's English daily.

So what then? Well after getting home and spending a couple of weeks enjoying the rapidly improved communication with Sveta, Joe very sensibly decides he must go back and have more face time with this lady. So he books another two weeks there, and after that they decide to have a week's holiday together in Egypt as their third meeting. In Egypt, Joe pops the question and Sveta accepts his proposal. All is well except for Joe's ailing bank account, he is feeling the pain. His two week jaunt cost him a further $5000 and the holiday in Egypt cost him about the same again. He paid for Sveta's flights, of course, but he got a good deal with the resort.

Joe bought Sveta a tasteful diamond engagement ring that cost him $3000 and she was his! Joe's total outlay, up to this point of being engaged, is nearly $31,000 and she has never even seen his home country yet. His next move could be to try getting her a much-coveted visitor visa to the US so that she can see his country and his lifestyle. That is easier said than done, therefore, he chooses to dispense with that step and head straight to the fiancée visa stage.

How Much Will This Cost Me?

Joe has not moved yet onto visa fees, the cost of the wedding and several subsequent trips to Belarus while the very slow wheels of American bureaucracy turn to process her fiancée visa. Relocation costs, settling in costs, dental, car, insurances, etc. have yet to be factored in. Joe could well end up having spent $100,000 before his Sveta is installed in his life and the big expenditures are behind him.

Americans have a fascination with gleaming white teeth and are more attentive to dentistry in general than are people from some of the other countries. Europeans and others are rapidly catching on to the desirable Hollywood smile, of course. Women from FSU countries seldom have this too high on their priority list as living expenses are high enough for them already. Dental care is usually considered only when one feels pain or has a specific problem. Many men factor into their expenses post relocation dental costs. Many Americans with whom I am acquainted have proudly announced that their new wife's gleaming white row of teeth cost them anywhere between $5k and $20k. It is not unheard of for some of the more impecunious of chaps to attempt to surreptitiously examine their potential women's teeth, hoping to mitigate this expense in advance. (I kid you not!)

Australians and Canadians can expect similar expenses to our hypothetical friend Joe above if they follow a similar route. British and mainland European men can save money with a few aspects if they do some bargain hunting with flights. The very savvy European sometimes finds a woman from the Baltic States who already possess an EU passport, thus eliminating visa fees altogether. Some men choose to target only women who speak English to remove the cost of English lessons, interpreters and translators from their calculations. Irrespective of whether or not English lessons are necessary, this endeavor usually requires a fat wallet, as you have no doubt gathered. What you gain in minor economies may well be eaten up later on by unexpected expenses.

Not everyone follows the same route; some people manage to spend a fraction of what Joe spent. Not all the money needs to be found at once of course, but seldom have I seen it successfully done on the cheap. I did hear about a man from Liverpool, England, who was in correspondence with a Russian woman from Riga in Latvia. When he checked flights he found a budget airline that served Riga direct from Liverpool Airport. He could get return flights for less than $250. The lady he was visiting, being from Latvia, held an EU Passport already so she didn't need a visa for England. This lady also spoke acceptable English which was soon developed with assimilation, so his bride hunt costs were almost the same as dating a local girl, except for his two-hour, bargain-basement flights that he chose to fund every other week. Not everyone can live in Liverpool and date a woman who is a direct, budget flight away, however.

There are no magic formulas to make this an economical experience. There are no agencies that offer any packages allowing you to both save lots of money and retain total choice and control, despite what they might claim. Of course, you can go with some full-service agencies and be railroaded by them into marrying the first woman you meet. I conversed with one agency owner who tries to coerce his clients into filling in a fiancée visa application after only a couple of chaperoned, stage-managed meetings within a few days of their arrival. Needless to say, I gave him a rather hard time about his particular business model.

How Much Will This Cost Me?

Avoid such short cuts to save money; it will end up a false economy. You cannot marry someone who you don't know, and you cannot know someone with whom you have minimal face-to-face contact. Attempting to save money at the outset may well come back to haunt you and will bite you twice as hard (especially in the divorce courts).

Into your reckoning you must factor the reality that she won't be working for some time after she arrives. Her ability to find employment will depend on her adaptation and on her language level. You owe it to these ladies, and yourselves, to get yourself settled and financially secured before even thinking of getting married to a Russian woman. Even when she does start work, she will not have the earning capacity that will help defray a fraction of the costs. Thus, she will be unable to significantly contribute to the household for the first two years of marriage. Her ability to make money should never factor in your survival budget, at least not for the next several years.

You can see, by now, that there is no definitive answer to the question of how much that this will cost. Asking how many angels could dance on the head of a pin would elicit a similarly accurate answer. I have tried to demonstrate both ends of the spectrum to you. What it will cost you will depend a lot on where you live, on where your target lady or ladies live and on how lucky you are. I suggest you start saving up now, you will need it.

I have outlined to you some of the future costs, which are not always apparent at first. It would be a crying shame to find a wonderful woman, who may be ideal for you, and to have to abandon the relationship because you were unable to fund your adventure to its conclusion.

If you are not too scared by the potential cost of your endeavor, we will look at what Russian women want from you and about the much-debated age-difference topic that you have probably been waiting for.

Chapter Four
Age Differences and
What Russian Women Want

Here we look at what Russian women want from you. Why do they look abroad for a husband? First, we will look at what Russian women who are already married to Western men say about why they wanted a Western man and what they like about us. Below are quotes from different Russian women married to Western men.

- "Western men are more family orientated."
- "The Western system protects women's rights. That makes men more responsible. Child support, alimony, etc., makes a man think twice before he runs out on his wife and children with no strings attached."
- "I was amazed to discover how gentle, how nice and caring he was."
- "They are calmer, more self-controlled, easy going, kinder and more caring than our local men."
- "Russian men did not see my education, which I had spent a good part of my life attaining, as being a beneficial part of my being."
- "Western men are different; they appreciate all of those little things which our men take for granted."
- "They do not dictate but discuss, our opinions seem to be important to them."

- "Russian men are always ready for a new adventure. They seem to be proud of having one more affair, while Western men normally do not consider having one if they are happy with their partner."
- "I was looking for a *serious* man." (A phrase you will encounter often.)

You will note in the above that none of the women expressed the desire for an old man. Age differences are a big issue for some men. We should look at Russian women's attitudes to large age differences first. The scenario of women with and without children should be examined separately, as women with and without children usually have different parameters with regard to age differences and what they are prepared to accept.

I personally know several men who are successfully married to knockout, childless women twenty-five or more years their junior. They are the exception rather than the rule and, curiously, those men usually do not recommend it to others. It is a fact that they are rather wealthy and it would be naive to suggest that this was not a contributory factor for the women. Some of these men have even had plastic surgery in an attempt to minimize the visual disparity between them and their young wives.

If a young, good-looking, childless woman is with an aged man it is because he has wealth. You will seldom see a different situation. Sometimes, you will see a young woman with an impecunious intellectual; academics do seem to attract a certain type of young lady. In the absence of excessive intellectualism, however, and the ability to express it in the Russian language, you large age gap seekers will have to rely on cold hard cash. If you are honest with yourself about it from the start, then a mutually satisfactory outcome could be possible. A self-delusional approach seems much less likely to end in happiness. Very seldom, if ever, do you see an age gap exceeding twelve to fifteen years with a good-looking, childless woman, in a lasting relationship, where the man is not somewhat affluent.

The old saying that wealth and experience buys youth and beauty is as true today as it has ever been, all that changes is the mode of demonstration of wealth. Given the relative ease with which we can traverse social and economic distance nowadays, the relative amounts of wealth and experience required to attain the goal may be reduced in the FSU. If you disagree with this, ask yourself why do you not date women who are twenty years younger than yourself at home?

Many women in Russia are open to a larger age difference than is common in the West. To understand this we need to look into Russian society a little. Contrary to agency rhetoric, most Russian women do not actively seek a very large age gap. They prefer a man to be up to ten and perhaps fifteen years (at a push) older than them. That is the most sought after and agreeable difference. Seldom will a Russian woman seek a younger man as they consider that a younger man will be unreliable, won't have serious intent, life and sex experience or the means to provide for a family.

Unfortunately, there are still some women who have altogether darker motives in this endeavor. There are parts of the FSU that are still extremely poor and the women there sometimes have zero prospects of improving their life. A fast exit funded by someone else is their only achievable self-betterment strategy in life, and it must be executed while they are still young and pretty enough to pull if off. These women are often likely to accept situations that other women wouldn't, such as improbably large age gaps or gaping chasms of incompatibility in the looks department.

A startlingly beautiful, super-slim twenty-one-year-old *does not* seek a sixty-year-old man with a paunch and a bald spot. Do not believe agency hype in this regard; it doesn't happen with genuine women. Such age gaps do happen of course, but usually only when the woman considers the European or US residence rights and potential future divorce settlement more attractive than the man mentioned above.

If seeking a very large age gap, you must consider the future when she is bopping around the house listening to the latest dance music eyeing the young muscular gardener through the window and you are dozing in your rocking chair with Bing Crosby oozing out of your stereo. It happens; what do you think will happen next?

If you are seeking a huge age gap, you must consider what kind of life you can give a young, beautiful Russian lady twenty to thirty years your junior. I doubt she'll have too much fun sitting at home watching television, or socializing with your peer group talking about the good old days or about their deteriorating health.

Consider the funny looks that she will receive from people as she walks around with you. Yes, you will be seen as lucky by other men while she is looked upon with scorn for being a gold digger or with pity for being so desperately poor that she had to settle for marrying her grandfather. She will watch young people go about their lives, young men, who she is attracted to, building their careers and other young people getting

Age Differences and What Russian Women Want

together for activities that you don't enjoy anymore. She will be jealous of young couples who can barely keep their hands off each other due to natural chemistry. Would you wish that on a woman? Switch the Bing Crosby back on and think about that for a while.

If seeking a huge age gap, how does this tie in with any June Cleaver-esque fantasies that you may have? A woman in her thirties or forties is more likely to be cooking apple pie; a woman in her twenties quite often will not cook anything, much less be domesticated. If she lives with her parents, her mother will have been doing most of the chores.

Some young women who still live with their parents can't even make a slice of toast and, increasingly, as Russia changes, many don't want to. Many women in their twenties actually imagine marrying an old foreigner will mean they will have servants to do the menial stuff. After all, if she marries an old man, what's in it for her? She will subconsciously want to be compensated for the compromise that she has made. That means a *very* easy life, which costs a lot of money.

In Russia, as with anywhere else in the world, women want to be with a man who looks credible with her and whom she finds attractive. This is actually a more important factor than the year on your respective birth certificates. If she is only looking for men up to forty and you are a young-looking forty-five-year-old in good shape, approach her and see what she makes of you, she may think you look like a worthy prospective partner. Most successful couples with large age gaps are due to a good balance between the partners' appearances.

Visual credibility is something that must be considered by you at the outset with any particular woman. Yes of course you want a hot younger woman, but how hot are *you*? If the answer is "not very" or "not sure," then ask yourself what motivation does a much-younger, good-looking woman have to get involved with you? If you are happy with money as an answer then do keep chasing those model-looking girls in their twenties, by all means. One of them will surely marry you for a couple of years.

If you want a significantly younger woman with genuine motivation, then consider the visual credibility. Let me spell it out - find a plainer girl who doesn't look like a model if you want a much-younger wife. I am not suggesting you go looking for ugly women, but I am suggesting that you accept your credible limitations with looks. Isn't the large age gap enough of a disparity without tempting fate yet further?

Of course we all want a younger woman, that and slimness are primary motivators for men to look in the FSU for a bride, but how far can one go with age gaps? I am often asked this question. The safe rule of thumb as regards age gaps with childless women is generally regarded to be that up to ten years is no issue, ten to fifteen years is okay if you are in decent physical shape, preferably in possession of your own hair and teeth and can pay the bills every month.

Beyond fifteen years, you are moving proportionately towards dangerous territory; the bigger gap you seek, the more dangerous it becomes and the healthier that your bank balance must be. Twenty years would be the realistic absolute maximum. That is the top and bottom of what is generally doable in age gaps with good-looking, childless women under age thirty-five. You should consider other seemingly well-presented opinions at your peril. If you take nothing else from this book, take this piece of advice.

Age Differences and What Russian Women Want

The general rules above can sometimes be stretched a little bit as women get older. The older a woman gets, the smaller her available pool of men becomes, and so the bigger the age gap that she is forced to accept. When a woman is over forty, circumstances are considerably different. She may have ideas of a man up to age fifty in her mind. However, a fifty-year-old man can meet a thirty-five-year-old woman with ease, so the older woman will quite probably have very few suitors in her ideal age group. What this means is, that by the time she reaches forty-five, the rules are thrown out of the window if she *looks* forty-five. In this scenario, a sixty-five-year-old man can often reasonably credibly marry a forty-five-year-old woman. A sixty-five-year-old marrying a forty-year-old, despite the twenty-five-year gap, is not unheard of and just about credible due to the mechanics that I have just outlined. Yet, the same twenty-five-year age gap, when projected onto a woman of twenty-five and a man of fifty, becomes rather incongruous and somewhat unlikely to produce a union that happened for the right reasons.

As a broad rule of thumb, with slim, childless, good-looking women under thirty-five, the size of your wallet needs to correlate proportionately with the size of age gap that you are seeking when it exceeds ten years. The bigger the age gap you seek, the more likely you will encounter gold diggers and passport hunters. It is possible to find a significantly younger woman if you are very discerning, and if you can manage to think with the big head rather than the little one. You should be prepared to make a *small* compromise in the looks department if necessary.

I can condense my advice about age differences with childless women into a nutshell, now that I have explained why it is so. If you are in your twenties, stay at home and get some experience with local women first, then come back in ten years. If you are in your thirties, look for girls from twenty-four to thirty-five. If you are in your forties, look for girls from twenty-seven to thirty-five. If you are in your fifties, look for women from thirty-five to forty-five. If you are in your sixties or above, look for women over forty. If you are seeking to meet girls aged eighteen to twenty-three, you should be cautious. More than likely she will only be looking to fleece you or to take you to restaurants and nightclubs so you can pay for her fun. She knows the price of her youth and beauty and it's not cheap. Don't date very young girls if you have serious intent, seldom are they mature enough to make rational informed decisions on important subjects such as leaving Russia forever to get married.

So what about women with children? If you are not seeking the legendary size-zero Barbie doll and will consider a woman the next size or two up (and I don't mean obese), or *especially* one with a child, this is the other side of the coin, the pool of younger women will begin to widen a lot more.

If you are happy to consider a woman with a child, (which means being prepared to adopt her child and be a proper father) then you can stretch the age advice above more often. Women with a child are much easier to find than women without, because in Russia it is very difficult for women with children to find a man that will take care of her and her child. In many cases these women are very motivated to meet a foreign man and to make the marriage work as she will also be thinking of a better future for her child and the stability that a family environment will offer for the child.

Age Differences and What Russian Women Want

A woman with a child may adapt easier abroad because then she will have her child to care for and this will keep her attention away from missing Russia. The only caveat with this route is that if a mother seeks residence abroad for her child, unless she has sole custody, she will usually need the father's permission for this, if he is around. However, many people overcome this hurdle by means of a traditional bribe to the father ($1500 being the going rate) to encourage him to sign the paperwork in a lawyers office. Sometimes, a Russian lawyer can *arrange* the letter of permission, persuade a court that the father cannot be found or one of several other creative routes. Russia is still extremely corrupt and everything… and I mean absolutely everything… has a price.

A sensible man must seek to establish quite early on how involved an FSU father is in his child's life. Often the answer is not at all. If there happens to be a responsible father on the scene, however, consideration must be given to the morality of the idea of removing a child from the father against his wishes. That is an aspect of this endeavor that you must work out in your own head based on your personal moral standards.

Russian women who are mothers also know that their available dating pool is significantly reduced because of their single parent status. This usually has two effects, first being that she will put her maximum effort into making the relationship work, as she is not only uprooting herself but her child. Failure is unthinkable. The second consequence is due to this shrunken dating pool, she may already be accustomed to widening her parameters about age gaps before she considered looking abroad. A rule of thumb is that you can add five years or so to my age gap advice with childless women if the lady has a child. That would suggest twenty-five years as the absolute maximum age gap that you should be looking at with a woman who is thirty to forty years old.

Nature dictates that exceptionally beautiful women will always have a larger selection of men from which to choose, compared to their less-spectacular sisters. These women will have greater opportunities in life, especially outside Russia. They are well aware that their sexual attractiveness is the hottest commodity in the international marketplace. Under these circumstances, it is not surprising that some of them milk it for all that it is worth and don't concern themselves with character or morality issues. Some women know the price of their beauty and their youth, as mentioned before. This brings us nicely around to the subject of money again.

The economic factor as motivation for *some* woman looking abroad cannot be underestimated. Much of the FSU is quite poor, compared to the West. Since the collapse of communism, the standard of living in the FSU has been increasing but tremendous disparity still exists. As an example, consider two former Soviet countries: Belarus and Estonia.

Estonia is now in the EU and is becoming more affluent every year; living standards there are comparable to any European country now. Belarus, on the other hand, still looks like much of Russia in many ways. Mile after mile of bleak monolithic high rise tower blocks, designed for Soviet workers, set against a grey polluted landscape. The results of the great socialist experiment are very apparent there and it almost drains the humanity from you when you are in such a place.

A poor girl from Belarus may indeed seek relocation to Florida, with Florida rather than the man being her primary motivation. Some men seek to exploit this economic disparity by looking in the poorest corners of the FSU such as Moldova and Ukrainian villages, in the belief that this financial leverage can get them a prettier and younger woman. I know a chap who calls this phenomenon *maximum economic exploitation*. Sometimes it works and an exceptional woman can be had, even if it does have a somewhat hollow feel about it.

However, an average Russian woman from a more affluent area is unlikely to seek to *reduce* her standard of living by moving to the West. Such a woman may legitimately quiz you more than you are comfortable with about your finances. Unfortunately, women who will scam you will ask similar questions under the same guise.

It is human nature to want to improve your life; Russian women are no different in this regard. It is a fact that many women choose the country or region that they will consider meeting men from, before they communicate with any men. This does not make them gold diggers. A woman only wants to relocate once. When she does, she will be leaving her homeland, family, job, friends and everything familiar in her life behind. She does not want to do this to live in poverty; she can do that very well at home. She wants to know that you can comfortably support her.

She needs to be absolutely certain that her new life abroad will present her with happiness, contentment and the opportunity for personal growth. The location, in addition to the man, is integral in that package. In that context, location should be chosen first. The fact that a woman will sometimes write that she is not interested in meeting men from the US, for example, shows that she has given it some thought. Often she will have considered the possibility of visiting her parents in the future and, to some, the US is perceived as too far away and too expensive for travel.

Most women attempt to seek out rich men in Russia and elsewhere. Men from abroad are in reality second choice to Russian men, a compromise, if you like. It makes perfect sense that this should be so if you think about it. If you could find what you wanted at home, you wouldn't be looking in Russia; it's the same in reverse. That said, there are many women who have married a foreigner who claim that they eschewed the company of all their peers. But cynics suggest if they had a string of suitors each capable and willing to offer a gilded and stable lifestyle in Russia, they would not have looked abroad in the first place.

It is not so much shallow moral standards that fuel the search for a rich man as you may expect, rather the socio-economic landscape of post-Soviet Russia. The transition to a market economy has unleashed a strong wave of consumerism with vastly exaggerated attention paid to clothes, cars, houses and visible signs of wealth, irrespective of whatever poverty underlies the thin veneer of glamour.

Appearance is everything to many people in Russia. The means for a woman to attain this lifestyle is usually afforded by an older man, a sponsor or a criminal. These factors, added to the belief that an older man may be a gentleman and know how to treat a woman, allows age gaps to be quite common. You will note again that age and money seem inextricably yet subtly linked together in the Russian psyche. A primary motivator for a woman seeking what she defines as a rich man is that she seeks a man with the ability to provide for a future family. In the uncertain society that Russia is, this is quite understandable.

Age Differences and What Russian Women Want

It is worth noting that, often, a Russian woman's perception of rich does not mean a Ferrari, four houses and a trust fund, it means, quite simply, *not poor*. As a foreigner, you are probably already by her definition not poor; thus you are perceived as rich already. A man who has a steady income, enough for all the necessities with a little left over every month, and who can afford a late-model car, for example, will be substantially richer than many of her local Ivan's. Therefore, by her definition, he is [you are] rich. Do not discount a woman if her profile says something like "I am looking for the successful man." She will probably mean a man who is employed and who can provide adequately for a family. Additionally, a successful man usually possesses certain social skills and a decent education. These are attractive traits to women of any nationality; Russian women are no exception.

In Russia there are *slightly* more women than men. Numerous military engagements, ill-health and alcoholism have all taken their toll. Often women claim that they can't find a *suitable* single man, so they often settle for being the mistress of a married man, accepting passing relationships or, indeed, looking abroad.

Being a married man's mistress does not carry the same stigma it does in the West. Often a knowing wife will choose to ignore her husband's infidelity lest she end up single herself once more. The mistress is content to have a man in her life and the gifts and treatment that are typical for a mistress.

Russia also has a tradition of what is referred to as sponsorship. In this situation, the affluent man, usually older and probably married, takes a younger mistress for a relationship. He provides her with an apartment and money for some of her living expenses, or sometimes just money. She in turn makes herself available for his discreet fun. Some of these arrangements go on for many years and the thought or intention of marriage never crosses either of their minds.

The woman in this scenario provides her body in exchange for a certain lifestyle. There seems little difference between sponsorship and prostitution in Western eyes. The subtle difference is that the sponsored woman usually has just the one sponsor, and occasionally a younger boyfriend or two as well. However, some women have multiple sponsors and indeed on free Russian dating sites that I have seen; up to half of the women are seeking sponsorship only. Some even specifying amounts that are acceptable to them each month.

Sponsorship is indeed a grey area where the lines between professional dater, prostitute and sponsored women are sometimes rather indistinct. Many women do not envision a future in this situation. Some of these women start to look abroad when they feel they are nearing the end of their shelf life as a sponsored woman, which is generally over the age of thirty. That could be referred to as a retirement plan really.

In reality, you would probably never know if you had met such a woman. Indeed, she would be hardly likely to volunteer such information to you. Asking searching questions on this topic would more than likely get you dumped and having such information would not benefit you anyway.

It is better to judge a woman on the experiences that you personally have with her and not to try to retrospectively impose Western morality onto her. Some would suggest that a marriage, where the woman accepts

Age Differences and What Russian Women Want

a very large age gap, is nothing more than de facto acceptance of a single permanent foreign sponsor.

One differential factor between Russia and the West is that almost all women ultimately want to have a husband and a family. Self-empowered, man-hating feminists are thin on the ground; the concept of a woman choosing to stay single is almost laughable. Most Russian women say that a woman needs a man to complete her soul.

Russian women *ideally* like to be married before they are thirty. After this time, they fear being left on the shelf and having to endure their family, co-workers and friends constantly asking them when they will meet a nice man and be married. There can be quite considerable social pressure on a woman over thirty to hurry up and to find a decent man for marriage, lest people think there is something wrong with her, or worse, that she may actually choose to remain single like those awful Western feminists that they all read about.

It is a fact, odd to us perhaps, that a woman in her mid-thirties, especially a divorced one with a child, is highly unlikely to find a decent husband in Russia, however beautiful that she may be. Russian men are usually very reluctant to take on another man's child with the financial burden that goes along with it.

There remains the belief that the good men are married young and the lucky wife who is married will hang on to him and his faults with her ten beautifully manicured claws. Better put, for women who are single after thirty, available men are not the same as eligible men. Similarly, eligible men are not the same as desirable men. The latter are very few, and female competition is extremely high for them; this is another reason Russian women look abroad.

Russian women often become disillusioned with their local men, not due so much to them swimming in an ocean of cheap vodka as you may read elsewhere, but due to their attitude to women. Sexual equality has not yet reached Russia with any vigor and many men display a bad attitude to women, often preferring frequent nights out with the boys chasing other, probably younger women, than behaving moderately and having respect for one woman.

Russian women cite Western men as being rather chivalrous and they consider us cultured, educated, responsible gentlemen who are mostly sober. Such a man is a good prospect for a husband. It is no secret amongst these women that men are flying in droves to the FSU to meet and marry women. A woman in her late-twenties or early-thirties knows that this relative youth she has is prized by men abroad, while in Russia she is nearing the end of her shelf life.

Foreign men tend to have a healthier lifestyle than Russian men and this makes a fifty-year-old Western man often in better shape, with a longer life expectancy than a forty-year-old Russian man. This touches once more upon an aspect that I covered earlier - looking credible together. It could be argued that Western affluence has the ability to make some men *seem* younger because they can afford quality healthcare, gyms, good clothes, etc., however, the fact that some can also often afford multiple luxury cars and several homes cannot be overlooked as a potential contributory factor for some women either.

Another fact, seldom discussed elsewhere, is the criteria that a man must meet to be considered suitable for marriage. In the West it is gener-

Age Differences and What Russian Women Want

ally accepted that you meet a partner, get to know them, fall in love, and after a considerable courtship you may consider marriage. This is not always so in Russia. There, a woman seeks primarily a *good man*, as detailed above. Whether she loves him or not can often be quite secondary. If they are mostly compatible, look credible together and he is a good man, he is marriage material.

Of course, love is ideal but, if everything else is in place, love will hopefully follow later. A Russian woman does not find it a deal breaker if she can't tick all of the boxes of her ideal man. If most of them are covered, she will often overlook one or two that he hasn't got. (She can work on those later.) You must not consider a Russian woman shallow to possess this mentality. She is a product of her country, culture and environment. One merely adheres to that which is familiar when no suitable alternatives are available.

A good man need not be amazingly handsome, either. As long as he isn't scary ugly, and has reasonably good internal qualities, his looks can often be quite secondary (within reason). Men having a few extra pounds seem to do okay in Russia, as well, assuming that the extra weight is in moderation, is not a health issue and that the man carries it well.

Another factor that will determine if you are seen as a good man is if a woman perceives you as *greedy* or not. Greedy has a slightly different meaning to Russians and greedy men are abhorred. For one to be considered greedy by a Russian would sometimes be what we regard as sensibly economical. A man who openly counts the cost of things and especially who revels in the savings that he has made will be considered a greedy cheapskate. One who trawls from shop to shop hoping to save a little money would be equally regarded.

If you comment that something is expensive, but you have a lot of cash in your pocket, you are clearly greedy in a Russian woman's eyes. You have the cash in your pocket, yet you won't buy it? Many Russian women will not understand why not.

There remains a misunderstanding between our different concepts of the word *expensive* also. To a Westerner, expensive or dear means either overpriced or not good value-for-money. To a Russian, expensive means that you cannot afford it or do not have the money for it. (Or rather may have it hidden in a sock and are unwilling to spend it.) There is a marked difference between pricey and unaffordable to us, yet, if a man objects to something being expensive, he is often incorrectly labeled greedy. He is perceived as being a skinflint, a miser or just plain cheap.

Common social etiquette for Russians is to not discuss the price of things, especially in romantic situations. No woman wants a greedy man. A man need not be greedy only with money; selfish or inconsiderate behavior of any kind can indicate a greedy soul too.

History has taught Russians that the future can be uncertain, that banks cannot be relied upon as a safe haven for your money and that the future may not happen (if you got sick for example), so why would you plan for it? If a Russian has $100 in his pocket and he wants something that costs $100, he will buy it. The fact he may need that $100 in the future will seldom be a consideration to him; tomorrow may never come.

A woman who relocates abroad will eventually learn about financial planning and the true economy of your country (that we are not all super rich) and lose some of that mentality. She will soon be the one scanning the stores for discounts and bargain sales but, for now, she is only familiar with her culture, which dictates that greedy men or men who manifest any of the diverse variants of greediness are to be avoided.

Race and skin color is an issue that we must cover. If you are a black or dark-skinned man looking for a white Russian lady, you must be aware that many Russian women are extremely racist. Forget the politically correct propaganda and doctrines pedaled from birth in your country. Many Russian women simply will not entertain the idea of a black or dark-skinned man.

Most Russian women avoid Muslim countries when considering permanent residence. Cheap Russian package holidays to Egypt and Turkey sealed that fate; many men there refer to Russian women as *Natashas*, some of whom were known for their loose morals and propensity to befriend Muslim dark-skinned men. Sooner or later, they discover that many Muslim men's ideas about relationships differ very much from their own. (There is even a pop song called "Sam tee Natasha" [you're the Natasha], about some Russian women turning the tables on one of these men.) If a Russian woman tells you that she has lived in Egypt, Turkey, Greece or, more especially, one of the Arab countries, or has spent any significant time there, beyond one or two package holidays, and most especially if she speaks Turkish, Arabic or a Muslim language, it should be your sign to treat her with extreme caution. This is a red flag, warranting further investigation about her motives for being there. If you meet a knockout tall, slim, blonde woman from Russia who claims to have lived there most of her life but lists Arabic or Turkish an additional language, it is a fair bet you are corresponding with an ex-prostitute or, at least, a woman you don't want to introduce to mother.

The aversion to dark-skinned men is not total and is not all encompassing. Many women, who consider themselves to be more cosmopolitan, especially those who see dark-skinned people in life and on the street or whom have encountered them in educational establishments - Moscow women, for example - are more likely to consider a dark-skinned man. Indeed, some may view the concept as different, interesting or even possibly desirable. A black man in Russia will be challenged for sure, but with perseverance and a thick skin, he will find success. Don't bank on too much support from her parents if they are traditional Russians however. A black or dark-skinned man often must work much harder on the parents than the girl if the union is to be accepted by the parents.

A Muslim man will fare slightly better in the East of Russia, within or in areas that border any of the *Stan* countries than in Central or Western Russia. Many Muslim people are to be found in South-Central Russia, East Russia and Kazakhstan, Azerbaijan, Tajikistan, Uzbekistan, Turkmenistan, Kyrgyzstan and other former Soviet Republics and associated territories in the Muslim geographical area.

Most Russian women, as we think of them, will be white. Most of them will consider themselves Russian Orthodox Christians, even the ones who never set foot inside a church. As such, they will feel more affinity to men from Christian countries, primarily Europe, Canada, Australia and the US. Without wanting to start a religious debate, it is fair to say that most Christian faiths are not too far removed from each other. Given this, an Orthodox girl will feel more at ease with a man originating

Age Differences and What Russian Women Want

from any kind of Christian culture. A good example is that Russian Orthodox ministers easily give blessing for a woman to marry in a Church of England Anglican church and they recognize that marriage as totally legitimate and in the eyes of god and the Orthodox Church. This blessing makes an Orthodox girl feel much more comfortable.

In a nutshell, what Russian women want is a good, attentive, sober husband and father for her current and any future children. He should not possess too many bad habits or exhibit too much bad behavior, especially greediness. Russian women are characteristically attention seekers, the bulk of which should come from their husbands. In return, if you choose correctly, you can expect a loyal, faithful loving wife who will put her husband and family exceedingly high on her agenda, often before herself.

She will be the glue that holds her family together. She seeks a proverbial Alpha male (many will settle for a Beta) who is a good provider, who makes her feel like a woman and whose income may stretch to a few luxuries in life. She is very adaptable, she will bend over backwards to please her husband and expects no less in return. For these reasons you see men who are married to Russian women are often smiling, like they discovered a secret. They have - you are learning what it is and how to get it.

Chapter Five
Scams, Scammers and Sharp Practice

Scamming is basically the action of fraudulently depriving you of some of your hard-earned cash under false pretenses.

Unfortunately, scams are rife in the world of Russian international dating. Law enforcement within the FSU with internet crime is minimal at best, more usually non-existent, so fraudsters can operate without fear of detection. Below I will demonstrate the more popular ones you are likely to encounter on your perusal of what can be, a very dirty barrel.

The first lesson to learn before you even choose a site to facilitate communication is to beware of *Hairy Boris*. Hairy Boris is a name applied to the many unscrupulous people in the Russian dating internet fraternity. Also referred to as *Fat Yuri* or *Sly Sergey*, he is everywhere, he is a scammer, he is sometimes actually female! We will call him Hairy Boris.

Hairy Boris is sometimes to be found working in dating agencies; he is more often found sitting behind a computer at home which can be in Moscow, Massachusetts, Marrakech or Manchester. He is clever. He will often contact you first either on a dating site or sometimes by posting a topic on a non-related forum urging contact. Sometimes his broken English language e-mail will just land uninvited into your mailbox. He has many ways to find you, you may have already heard from him. Names, e-mail addresses and photographs are all fungible of course.

He will claim to be a Russian woman seeking love, often *she* will post or send pictures and *she* will always give you an e-mail address. At the point you reply, *she* will suck you in with tried and tested psychological tricks. The first e-mail will be all about *her* job, life, hometown, parents, friends, etc. This will be to paint the picture of a nice girl. Many questions will be, "Tell me about you?" In your reply you will tell Boris all about yourself. *She* will then tell you how compatible that *she* thinks you both are. By the third or fourth e-mail, *she* will be professing feelings for you in romantic terms, highlighting a desire to come to you ("arrive to you" is the usual phrase) and speaking of your future together.

At this stage is where the scam kicks in. The scam will be in the form of a request for money. Usually to buy tickets to come to you, pay for a visa, pay for healthcare for *her* or poor sick old mother. *She* will possibly e-mail you scans of tickets or visas that she claims to already have, or anything that you want. Boris knows how to use Photoshop software. Often a scammer will claim that *she* already has a visa to your country and is planning to come on holiday or to study already.

By now you will be convinced you are dealing with a real woman and reading this you may laugh out loud, but untold thousands of men have fallen for these scams and sent money, usually by Western Union or a similar service. And most don't tell. Boris is safe to move on to the next victim. Hairy Boris and his cohorts are sophisticated and clever criminals. Often their communications are structured and pre-written by psychologists as a series so they must only change the names in the e-mails, and they even use computer programs to do that.

A real Russian woman will never want to come right over and visit you and spend an indeterminate amount of time with you. She will write fairly short letters and not have gushing, one-sided conversations with herself like Boris does. A real Russian woman mostly keeps her true feelings to herself until she has determined that she has met a real decent man in person. That doesn't happen overnight, it takes time.

The main lesson here is to never send money to someone who you have never actually met for healthcare, visas, tickets, flights, unforeseen emergencies, rent or anything of that nature. Never send any money for anything unless the women has been verified as totally genuine, preferably by a native Russian speaker - your independent interpreter/translator perhaps - and you are in serious communication. By this, I mean a woman you are in frequent telephone contact with and whom you have all contact information for. *Never* send money to people who are *only* e-mail correspondents. A genuine woman will never ask you for money, at least not until you have met face-to-face.

Beware of anti-scam sites, honest agency listing sites, certified accreditation schemes, anti-scam banners, fancy seals on websites and other nonsense of that genre. They are often meaningless and you will never know which are and which are not. Agencies often must pay to be listed on anti-scam and accreditation sites, and agencies that don't pay are often blacklisted, rather akin to internet extortion. Many of these self-appointed agency world cop schemes are set up by the agencies, forum owners or others who only want to make money or to discredit competitors and enemies.

A long, slow read of a good internet forum devoted to Russian women and their pursuit thereof, will find accounts from men, actual customers, who have used particular agencies and of men who are married to women whom they met through these agencies. These are much better recommendations than a fancy looking seal on a website or some site proclaiming, "We support anti-scam, etc." Often the agencies that preach the loudest are the very ones that have employees who double up as Hairy Boris to fleece you of your cash or who run unscrupulous schemes or translator frauds.

It is an unfortunate fact of life that some of the biggest agencies out there are scam agencies. If you type "Russian wife" (or a similar phrase) into Google, many of the huge agencies that you will find on page one and two are purported to be the biggest culprits. How to choose an agency is covered more in the next chapter but do not be lulled into a false sense of security by going with a big agency; some will be fine and some won't. You cannot judge if an agency is a scam agency by its size. You will find links to some of the better-regarded agencies on our exclusive resources website detailed at the back of the book.

I heard recently a tale involving a big agency that has a very good reputation around the various forums, mostly by virtue of the owner knowing the forum owners themselves, but there are also some client accounts of good experiences with this agency. Then I heard an account about an American man who sent $75 to this agency to deliver some flowers to the lady he was corresponding with; a simple enough task one would imagine. So, did the agency buy and deliver the flowers? No. What they did was offer the lady the option between flowers or $10; she chose the money. Then they all went to the flower stand kiosk, a bunch of flowers are momentarily rented for the princely sum of $1, photographs are taken of smiling girl holding the rented flowers, she makes $10, the Agency makes $64 and the man gets his photographic proof of flower delivery.

The same scam with minor variations is often applied to gift delivery and English lessons which men are encouraged to pay for through agencies. This said; there are many honest agencies who would not contemplate such a tactic. I generally recommend avoiding overpriced agency flowers and gifts when one can usually either send direct or source through a reputable specialist supplier.

The same man involved with the $10 flower girl above amazingly went on to visit and meet the girl in her hometown. Despite the fact he had been writing to her for months, her first detailed knowledge of him was twenty minutes before his arrival when the agency contacted her and told her she was meeting a man. He was naturally surprised that she had no recollection of the many letters that they had exchanged. Of course, he later found out he had been writing to an agency translator, who was confident that, since only an estimated 5-10 percent of men who write actually arrive, the scam was safe and the translation money would keep rolling in. Sorry Boris, not this time!

Men who arrive in similar circumstances sometimes find the women are inexplicably unavailable or out of town at a family crisis, which translates as they refused to be complicit in the fraud, even for a kickback. So the man does not waste his trip, the agency then charges him much more money for short notice introductions to supposedly serious girls who are available tonight and who are exceedingly complicit.

Some would speculate that such agencies have a shortlist of available girls who are only too eager to have a foreigner take them out to a restaurant and spend some money on them. It will, of course, be most unfortunate when the evening is interrupted by an urgent call from her sick old mother just before the awkward kissing is expected. If there is a possibility of milking the guy on a second date, perhaps to a local shopping center, such a woman may put a non-verbal suggestion of sex on the table. Naturally, these are professional daters who seek only to empty your pocket, not women you marry.

Another money-making scheme, practiced by unscrupulous agencies, is the availability of the women who they market. Often when a woman is in serious communication with a man she will request that her profile be removed (or at least tagged as unavailable). Some agencies not only refuse to do this but continue to bombard her with new communication from other men, or sometimes write letters of reply to the men themselves. I have even heard of one agency that physically threatened a woman and her family when she asked to be removed because she had met a local man. She was very attractive and they sold her contact details often. In Russia, money talks.

Once you begin a direct e-mail communication, and you have removed the agency from your communications (as you should seek to do at an early stage), one of your first routine checks should be the IP address. The IP number is like a computers address, it usually correlates to the region or city where the computer was that the e-mail was sent from. The IP address is to be found in the jumbled mass of nonsense at the top of, or attached somehow to an e-mail. In that jumble somewhere, you will find some numbers punctuated by stops. A typical example would be 195.161.246.35. This is an actual scammer's IP that I once assisted an American attorney to expose; his real name was, in fact, Boris! There will be several such IP numbers in there, some belonging to innocent e-mail servers, find the one that is labeled *originating IP*. If in doubt, check all of them. One should identify her general vicinity.

To check them find a website to trace IP addresses such as dnsstuff.com. Put the number in the search box and it will usually give you the country, if not the city of origin. If that is close to where the woman claims to live, then all well and good. If not, you need to do some more sniffing. Next, Google just the IP number to verify that it has not been published on any scam sites. Again, that is only a hint and reading is required as in Russia whole districts can have the same IP address.

Never rely exclusively on these methods to flush out a fraud as they are not totally infallible methods. Some results will be inconclusive or not close enough. Outright frauds will often display IP numbers in totally different locations. However, if a woman who claims to live in Moscow e-mails you from a Russian e-mail server, such as mail.ru or yandex.ru, but her IP address corresponds to a distant city or country, you can be quite sure you have met Hairy Boris again.

This is another note about e-mail headers. Amongst the jumble in which you will find the IP address, look for a reference to "The Bat!" This is a program that can be used to facilitate mass e-mailing, or spamming. It can be used to tailor specific automated replies to specific users, as well. Hairy Boris is quite fond of this program. The presence of "The Bat!" should not be considered to be conclusive however, because some internet cafés and companies use this program. It is seldom used on home PC's.

When you obtain full contact information for a woman, you need to remember that Google is your best friend. Knowing how to use this search program effectively will flush out the amateur or well-used scams in a moment. Whenever you think you might be getting scammed, you probably are. Google is a valuable resource and ought to be used as a routine matter of due diligence.

The anonymous nature of internet correspondence is the root of the scam problem really. Irrespective of whether one is in correspondence with a sincere woman or with Hairy Boris, the sooner that you progress to telephone conversations, the better. It is human nature that a person who is hopeful of a relationship will want to hear your voice. The last thing that a scammer wants to do is to spend hours on the telephone having soppy conversations with hopeful, ardent swains.

It happens often with a scammer that the *woman* who is your interlocutor will claim not to have a telephone. It most cases this is *not* true. Very seldom will a woman not have a telephone; many have a landline as well as a mobile. It is worth noting that a cautious woman may be reluctant to give out her number until she is convinced you are *the serious man*. In any case, treat with extreme caution women who claim that they have no telephone of any description.

How in the world would such a woman expect to engage in an international relationship without a primary means of communication? Also abandon all ideas that FSU ladies are too poor to buy a mobile phone, it is simply not true, many would rather not eat for a month so that they can have the latest model to pose with.

A classic excuse with scammers who claim to have no phone is the pre-arranged call. You will be given a *friends* number to call at a certain time, when it will be claimed that your interlocutor will answer. Hairy Boris will have merely procured a local woman, maybe his girlfriend, to pose as your woman. He hopes that the language barrier will prevent an in-depth conversation and the exposure of his scheme. A call by a native speaker, maybe an unannounced three-way call with your translator/interpreter, would expose this ruse in moments, of course. A native speaker will easily pick up on a hesitant woman who isn't giving the right kind of answers.

If your woman truly has no personal phone, she will have a work number, a parent, a friend or a neighbor who has one and she can be reached ad hoc via this method. Do not be fobbed off by the no-telephone gag. If you encounter too much resistance getting a number from a woman, it would be better to move on to one of many women who you can contact by telephone. If you get her house telephone number, check that out also. A lady from a particular city ought to have a corresponding city code on her landline. If she claims to be from Samara, for example, but her telephone number exhibits the city code for Vladivostok, you may just have busted Hairy Boris again. Google will help you in that regard also.

Almost every scam love letter has been copied and pasted over and over by Hairy Boris. He sends them out by the thousand. Many a gullible male recipient of those thousands has ultimately responded by sending money (usually by Western Union). Luckily for you, many of those defrauded men have been willing to share their experiences.

Names (all variations and also in Cyrillic), addresses, telephone numbers, profile numbers, and any other unique information should be

Googled. E-mail addresses are fungible, but can be an aid. To Google anything unique you should put double quotation marks on either side of it to only search for those words, numbers or characters in the order in which you have entered them. If searching randomly, just use her name, city and the word *scam* to see what sort of results that you get. Try many variations of search criteria and you will soon get very adept at it; it almost becomes a sport.

You are going to find a lot of women in the FSU with the same or similar names. More so if the name is a common one and transliterated into English. Names can have differences; Elena can be Lena, Helen, Hellen or Yelena, for example. Olga can be Olya, Olechka, Olenka or Olyushka. Most Russian women's names have several alternatives in common usage. Most Russians are traditional when naming children and don't tend to name their children *Rainbow, Fifi* or *Skye*.

Do not rely solely on names; try phrases from her letters too. If the target of your search has passed the first tests, phrases in the letters, which sometimes appear to have been written by a machine translator, or are in some other way unique, are your next most important resource. Place double quotation marks around six to twelve words in the letter that seem reasonably unique, strangely spelt or badly punctuated and enter them in the Google search engine. If those words lead you to a letter almost identical to yours on a scam site, then you have probably met Hairy Boris and are being set up to be scammed.

One small caveat about finding your woman on a scam site, however, is the content of what you find. If she comes up at twenty different sites by many different authors then the evidence is overwhelming and is seldom incorrect. However, if you just find one entry on a solitary forum or site, examine the report closely, also examine the previous posts of the author and see if many of his contributions are spitting venom at women.

It is a sad fact that many men who were merely rejected by women are so disgruntled that they go and write that woman up as a scammer somewhere to thwart her future attempts at happiness with a more suitable man. Always read the evidence presented and decide for yourself. Some sites will say, "X number of scam reports found with X name." When you click through they will ask you to pay to view this gripping, must-have information that they claim to hold; disregard and ignore such sites. They too are scams, scam sites scamming people searching for scammers!

A more subtle form of scam is the professional dater. You may end up visiting a professional dater and only then will you find out that her idea of a first date is for you to purchase her a new expensive mobile telephone or some such item. The next port of call may be to casually peruse the fur coat store, while she is draped all over you pouting, with faux longing in her eyes. Many a soft-hearted man has had his pocket emptied this way. She may even throw some sex into the deal to keep you spending while you are there, provided that you have passed the first-date test.

Some of these women will find subtle ways to avoid the sex for the week or so that you are there. Often, an obscure gynecological problem will be blamed, menstruation or some other physical condition. Sometimes, a well-timed argument, urgent appointment or tiredness will be the reason. Of course, a genuine woman can have similar issues that will interfere with sex or she may just simply not find you attractive.

As a rule of thumb, a woman should not ask you outright for anything of significant value until you are in a well-established relationship. That said, a perfectly decent Russian girl from a good family can hint, on a second date, that her spike heeled boots are too thin for the coming winter and will accept a new pair with no ambivalence clouding her sense of gratitude. This may be underpinned by a sense of entitlement, because you are the man, so it is your duty to make her warm. (Well, you wanted a traditional woman, didn't you?) It is a fine line that you may only recognize when you have been fleeced a few times and the physical side of the relationship is not really developing.

I heard recently an account of a man who was visiting a woman in Ukraine. While walking on the street on their first day together, they passed a big department store. The woman asked if he would mind buying her a lipstick. A lipstick is seldom an expensive item, he naturally agreed, they went into the store. While there, the one lipstick became three (as she couldn't choose a color) and a need for some matching eye shadow, eye liner as well as a bottle of perfume arises. It got rang up at the till and it was $300.

Perhaps she was testing him to see if he was greedy. After all, nobody wants to marry a greedy man. Maybe it was her subtle test to see if he was gullible, maybe she was genuinely quite poor and she thought that all foreigners are rich and the price was nothing to him. (This is a common misconception.) Perhaps she had got him there only to spend money before the next sucker came along. All of those things are possibilities, we shall never be certain. Was she a scammer, a professional dater or a normal woman? You decide.

The main unseen difference with a professional dater, despite that she will often be the agency's front page traffic-stopping girl, is that she will probably have two different men a month visiting her and absolutely no intention of ever leaving her country. This is nice work, if you can get it.

One of the only early defenses against such women is if one of the men who has gone before may have contributed their tale to a scam site or to an internet forum. Again, if you have been using Google, as mentioned above, you may have been forewarned and never have gone to visit her.

Passport hunters, known as *Green Card Girls* by the Americans are another hard group to spot. This breed will be completely available to create and nurture a relationship, she will want to get you there and she will want you to fall in love with her. This type of woman will jump through all of the hoops with only one objective: To get the hell out of her country and get foreign residence rights - preferably a foreign passport or at least a residence permit - as quickly as possible. Her intent from day one is to divorce you and move onward and upward, probably to a much younger man.

Early exit from a marriage after arrival on foreign soil is hastened in some unfortunate cases, usually in the US, by the woman falsely claiming domestic violence against her shiny new husband. She calls the police, he gets arrested, she is taken to a battered women's shelter and later re-housed, and resplendent with her new residence permit (Green Card) and divorce in progress. In some European countries and elsewhere, laws are in force that allows this same fraud to work there also.

So, how are you to protect yourself from such a woman? This part is difficult to advise on. You have to trust your gut instinct. You can look for what you consider to be red flags in her behavior. The biggest red flag would be that she is happy to marry a much-older man rather quickly whose league she far excels. Other typical red flags may include not introducing you to her best friends or to certain members of her family, especially parents. Maybe she will not discuss having children with you and may be fanatically careful about birth control. Others may be that she makes no effort to arrange long-term projects with you such as teaching you Russian or starting a business. Maybe she was the one who contacted you first or maybe not having been noticeably religious before, after she arrives, she wants to know where the Orthodox Church is right away and rushes meet the Russian people there to start networking. Some demand lots of gifts and get angry or moody if you say no, others have uncanny, in-depth advance knowledge about the immigration procedure or the domestic violence laws in your country.

The men who have been hoodwinked in this way often went to the FSU ready for love and romance but instead got taken to expensive overpriced restaurants, nailed for overpriced taxi fares from the woman's complicit boyfriends and taken on shopping sprees telling themselves love has no price and scared of saying no lest they be labeled greedy. (There's that word again!) If they dare to question her actions, she spins it around by questioning his love. It should not be like this. Only a man with the skill to think with the big head and not the little head can spot such a woman.

The possible red flags that I gave you above are far from exhaustive and, in and of themselves, are not enough alone to warrant labeling a woman a Green Card Girl. They are just a few possible examples of behavior out of many possibilities. There is no magic formula here except for common sense, knowledge and experience. I hope when you have finished this book, you are able to spot a passport hunter at fifty paces.

Apart from passport hunters and Green Card Girls, scamming is always about the short-term money and the most expedient way that either a professional dater or Hairy Boris can relieve you of some of yours. The most popular advice that you will hear on this subject is, "Don't send money." While excellent advice on the surface (and it is indeed true that if you never send any money you will never be scammed), it is advice mostly aimed at newbies to the international dating scene; those who Hairy Boris may fleece into coughing up a couple of grand for poor old mother's urgent operation or money to *arrive to you*.

I know of many situations where sensible, well-informed men have sent money to women who they haven't yet physically met - I don't recall any of them being scammed as a result. There is a big difference between sending money to a photograph of Hairy Boris after a few *I want to make the cozy home* e-mails and a sensible man, having established without doubt that the woman is genuine and having opened up all of the lines of communication, to send some money to facilitate something that will be beneficial to the developing relationship.

Most men who do send money do so to facilitate an internet connection, for the woman to commence English lessons without delay or for some other useful purpose. Perhaps she has to pay a deposit for the apartment that you rent when you visit or some other visit-related expense. Such an amount will not be very much in the grand scheme of things; it will be a few hundred rather than a couple of thousand.

It tends to be the men who can afford to send money who send it. As such, those men usually had to use their grey matter and judgment to acquire said cash in the first place. If the same good judgment is applied to the decision to send the money, scamming is unlikely. Any money you send should only be money that you can afford to lose. It becomes a gamble with the odds in your favor if you use common sense. You will enjoy much better odds than the Lotto or the roulette table. If the purpose was genuine, but the relationship doesn't work out, console yourself with the knowledge that your generosity may improve her chances to find a man with whom she can be happy.

In conclusion, sending money is sometimes justified if it's not too much and it is sent for a sensible, constructive purpose and, especially, if it is your idea. Never send money to a woman, unless you have established beyond a reasonable doubt that she is not Hairy Boris. You should be talking to her often. When I say *talking to her*, I mean just that. If you haven't spoken to her on the telephone, you are not talking to her. Moreover, you should be having regular telephone conversations to build your relationship, every day if possible.

Only after you meet the real woman, in person, and she doesn't try to scam you, will you have an idea that she is not a scammer. Even then, you may not know for sure straight away because there are passport hunters, professional daters and agency shills seeking to hoodwink you. All that you can do, as regards being scammed, is to follow the advice in this chapter, to do your early, due-diligence checks, to use your common sense, to think with the big head (rather than with the little, hungry one) and to trust your inner voice. If something doesn't smell right, it probably isn't right. Do not write off too many red flags as cultural differences. Remember that you are attempting to build a real relationship. If in doubt about something, ask yourself if you would accept this from a local woman or if you would do *this* or pay for *that* for a local woman. If the answer is no, then you should apply the same rationale if you are involved with a Russian woman.

The Latin phrase *abundans cautela non nocet* means "abundant caution does no harm." Please remember it.

Chapter Six
How to Select an Agency or Contact Method

Undoubtedly you will be using the internet in your quest. I recommend avoiding chat media such as Yahoo, ICQ and AOL in the first instance. (Who has AOL in Russia anyway?) Also avoid video and blog type media to be found on sites like MySpace and YouTube. Direct personal advertisements, where anyone is invited to place a free profile, are also not recommended. They do not screen their members and many advertisements are Hairy Boris in disguise. Often in this media you find advertisements placed by Russian marriage agencies themselves. In this situation it is not uncommon to end up paying twice, first to join the contact site, then again to a local agency to actually contact the lady. Personal sites do not usually give you any direct contact details of the women; they only forward your e-mail to them. I will tell you how to do it all ways though.

The most reliable place for a man who is new to this endeavor to look for a Russian wife is a specialist Russian dating agency. The better ones screen their members and provide direct contact information of the women (postal address, e-mail address and phone number) at an early stage. When selecting an agency, choose one that fits your criteria and that is recommended by many sources, especially by clients on one or more of the internet forums for international dating. If the agency is disreputable, people on the forums will tell you about it.

Some agencies, which are known as address mills, only sell direct contact information of their women. Usually, they only provide postal addresses that can be years old and hopelessly out-of-date. Some require membership while others combine the two options. The average price of an address is $10 - $50.

Membership options vary between agency sites. Despite any variations, your benchmark should be, first and foremost, whether you can buy the ladies' actual direct contact information. Or, at least, is it available with the woman's prior approval after some contact or communication has taken place? If not, you should avoid these agencies because they are only cash cows for their owners. A good agency will sell you the contact information one way or another, sometimes with the ladies prior approval, and will thereafter allow you to pick and choose their services like a buffet.

Don't be shy, contact the owners before spending any money and ask directly what their policy is about obtaining ladies personal contact information if it is unclear from their website. If they don't reply, if they reply evasively or with ambiguity, you assume the worst and avoid them like the plague.

By now you should have done some homework on where you want to look. The FSU is a very big place and where you live may be a factor as to a reasonably priced destination. Many Americans seem to prefer Ukraine as they can travel visa free to there, and there is much US-friendly support, as well. Many British men and Europeans prefer Russia because they feel that the extra effort expended in getting a Russian visa is offset by the competitive advantage since most Americans search in Ukraine. Many men prefer lesser-trod places such as Georgia and Kaliningrad. Be aware that in much of the east of Russia and in Uzbekistan, Kyrgyzstan,

How to Select an Agency or Contact Method

Tajikistan, Kazakhstan and Azerbaijan you will find predominantly Muslim women.

Muslim women (unless you are a Muslim man) will find it very hard to adapt to a mostly Christian-based society as exists in the West. Most Russian woman we are talking about will be from Central and Western Russia, Ukraine, Belarus, Latvia, Lithuania, Estonia, Kaliningrad, Armenia and Moldova. Although there are many multi-ethnic areas of the FSU where Orthodox Christians and Muslims happily coexist, and within those areas you will find Western looking moderate Muslims alongside others who may regard you as the infidel. Don't be put off so much by area. Find *the look* of the woman you want, be it Slavic, Tatar or whatever flicks your switch, and select agencies in the regions that have the most women who suit your fancy. The FSU is a land of contrast, where you will find mini-skirted, olive-skinned Muslim girls as well as pale-skinned, Slavic Christian girls in the same city.

Whatever your taste, you have to do your homework and determine what basic physical type of lady that you want in your life and where she is likely to be found. If you prefer the Slavic/Scandinavian-looking, blonde-haired, blue-eyed lady, you should look in Estonia, Latvia, Lithuania, Ukraine, Belarus and Western Russia. But don't rule out a woman in Georgia whose family may have relocated years ago. Russia is indeed a land of contrast and people can't always be found where you expect to find them.

The most straightforward and least-expensive way to begin your search is to find a site where you just buy mailing addresses. In this case, you must write postal letters. They can take many weeks to arrive to a communal mailbox and to their intended recipient. (Sometimes, they never arrive.) Be advised that many profiles and photographs on such sites may be several years old and completely obsolete. After a first letter sent this way, if you follow my *how to write the first letter guide*, you may well end up with full contact details early on. However, with the snail-mail introduction method from such sites, you should expect a response rate of approximately 5-10 percent. This is a slow and inefficient method for sure, but it is not one to be discounted.

My personal preference is for small, harder-to-find, family-owned agencies where you can interact with the owners and build a rapport. The owners often know the ladies personally and they have a good idea what the individual lady likes and dislikes. They will be more honest with you than a big, profit-driven agency. Small agencies, even if based in England or the US, will often be run by a married couple and many of the women profiled will be the wife's friends from back home. Given this she would be able to say with confidence, for example, that Svetlana would really prefer an Englishman or that Olga would not consider a black man.

If you feel that you need it, you can find what is known as a *full-service agency*. Such agencies will handle everything including orchestrating your meetings with several women, providing a translator, delivering gifts, arranging transport, booking your hotel and generally holding your hand through the entire process.

In my experience, when you use such an agency and rely on them to do so many things for you, it is all too easy to be steered toward meeting recommended women who have been coached to say the right things in your early meetings. Remember, they often do not want their homepage, traffic-stopping girls to get married as they are their cash cows who drag the customers in.

Accordingly, they will dissuade you from the über babes since they want the plainer ones to be married. (Then they get to plaster your photograph on their site as another success story.) Many full-service agencies target and indeed do attract the socially inept man. Sometimes these men end up married to women who they don't really know. (In time, they may wish that they didn't know them.) Being a client of a full-service agency usually requires very deep pockets.

Speaking of deep pockets, a few of the bigger agencies offer what they call tours or socials. The basic idea is to arrange to have a group of men fly out to an FSU city at which the agency books a party venue, which is usually at a club or at a restaurant. The agency will arrange airport transfers, hotel accommodations and a few other basics for a package price. Local women are invited to attend so that they can meet the men. They usually aim for attendance of many more women than men to make the men feel like they are bathing in Slavic beauties. These socials are marketed as economy pursuits for clever coves who want to get ahead of the game; *make one trip and meet fifty to one hundred women* is usually how they are touted.

On the face of it, that sounds reasonable, but when one delves a little deeper, one may form a different opinion. First of all, the men who attend these socials are often less than stellar as far as weight, appearance and social skills go. Socials seem to attract the men who need considerable hand holding by the agency. Socials also tend to attract a few sex tourists and biggest bang-for-the-buck merchants.

A perusal of any of the big sites' social/tour photograph galleries will provide you with photographic confirmation of the type of men who typically attend their functions. Men who feel more secure in the company of other men with similar aspirations are attracted to socials as well. (The herd mentality applies.) Roughly translated, that usually means Americans who have never traveled alone outside of the US.

Most women who I have met would not go near a social with a ten-foot rubber prophylactic. That being the case, one must question the type of ladies who will typically frequent a social. Often, one finds a mix of over-made-up forty-somethings, desperate to snag a rich American (or any American), a few will likely be overweight and rejected by traditional bride hunters. You will also find a few slim, attractive women, some of whom will be professional daters, hookers, good-time and party girls; and other delightful lovelies who are there for what they can get.

What they can get is free food, free drinks, and sometimes even a few quiet dollars from the hosting agency to encourage their timely arrival, being clad in something very short and skimpy and, better yet, bringing a friend or two with them. The percentage of nice, genuine women attending socials is quite small.

It is possible that a sprinkling of normal serious women may have been lured there by the agency's marketing ploys but they are thin on the ground and often leave early when they get the measure of the situation. I have no recollection of having met anyone who successfully married a woman who they met at a social. However, some agency websites are adorned with smiling couples who allegedly met at these things. I am sure some of these happy couples exist, but I have yet to personally encounter

How to Select an Agency or Contact Method

one of them.

Socials are good for agencies. Twenty to fifty men, at several thousand dollars each and multiple tour dates, with more men tagging on along the way, will provide the agency owner with a nice wad of cash. It also makes for great website pictures with which to lure more men to their socials in a self-perpetuating fashion. You should attend these socials at your own risk.

If the idea of a tour appeals to you, it should be with a provider that allows you access to the underlying sub-agencies and who assists you to get acquainted with the women by correspondence and telephone prior. I only know of one agency that operates this way with tours, you will find their link on our resources website.

Every agency uses a different business model, usually to maximize their income according to their circumstances. The agencies with in-house translators can sometimes be corrupt with the translators changing content of correspondence. The only aim is to keep the translated e-mail flowing and, of course, to get the men to visit and to pay for ancillary services.

It has been known, as mentioned earlier, for men to have exchanged many letters via agency translators but to discover later that the woman has no knowledge of their existence! The agency writes the letters merely to generate translation revenue in this circumstance. It is a much-touted figure that only 5 percent of men who write ever actually visit. Some agencies capitalize on this. This is why in-house translator fraud is so rampant, yet infrequently discovered.

For men who want to go it alone and run the gauntlet with Hairy

Boris, there are free methods available. There are some free contact sites that you can use, mostly in Russian language, but wading through all the spam and dubious characters one finds in such places is too much trouble for most. I do know men who met their wives through such sites, so sometimes this approach works. A website called Free Russian Personals is the main player in this area. The website love.mail.ru is another popular contender, although love.mail.ru has many women seeking sponsorship and/or only Russian men. On our resources website is a link to a page that will teach you how to navigate a Russian language, free-dating site should you want to.

Another free method, when you are feeling more experienced, is ICQ. With a bit of effort, you can confidently go where most men haven't even considered looking. Get a map of Russia and pick a city. Do a search for women in that city who are in your age range and who list English as a language. Leave the other criteria blank. Just click on the names and say hello. You will get some replies for sure.

But you can go further with this. Choose a city and do an internet search and you should be able to find that city's name in Cyrillic, or check your map if it has Cyrillic on instead. Type or copy and paste the Cyrillic city name into the ICQ search but still specify English as a language. You'll get many more results and here's the best part: Most of these women aren't featured on any agency, nor are they actively seeking a foreign man, until they meet one (that would be you). You'll find that most ICQ profiles have the bare minimum of information but, if a girl knows English, she will have that in her profile because she will be proud of it.

With a little work on your ICQ profile you can enter your ICQ num-

How to Select an Agency or Contact Method

ber in the dating section. You can then upload a photograph and add more information. The more information that you add, the more you'll show up when the Russian women are searching. If you can read and understand most of the letters of the Cyrillic alphabet, maybe know one hundred words and be able to translate using online translators, this *just* qualifies you by the skin of your teeth to include Russian as a language in your profile. The result will be that Russian women will contact you quite often.

ICQ is low bandwidth and works fine with archaic Russian dial-up internet connections. Many women can't afford to pay for the bandwidth required to surf the internet, find dating sites, post profiles, upload photographs, etc., but they can afford to use ICQ. Yes, it's free, but as with any free medium, you will find your fair share of spammers and scammers in there.

While there are seemingly thousands of agencies from which one can choose, many are connected to each other in a variety of ways. Some agencies are affiliates of others or they may be in a network of some type. This basically allows agencies to share profiles with each other in order to offer the client a wider choice (or simply to make more money, depending on your point of view). The difficulty with this is that all agencies have different policies and some are honest but some are not. It is hard to tie agencies together this way and expect uniform policies and ethics throughout the network.

Many agencies also trade under a variety of names utilizing the same databases across various websites, which, on the surface, appear to be unconnected, until you investigate. Agencies often sell each other profiles, as well. This explains why some women appear on twenty different sites, usually without their knowledge. This also explains why some agencies have thousands of women that would otherwise not be possible.

With network and affiliate type agencies, it is prudent to try to ascertain the identity of local agency in the town of interest. This will be the originating agency that signed her up in the first place. Going directly to that agency can often be cheaper than working through an affiliate and it gives you the opportunity to check that agency's reputation before parting with any cash.

So, if you find a woman in a smallish town listed on a huge agency, which is not based in that town, search for the small agencies that are in her town and check their women's galleries. You may well find her this way. It's always nice to know who you are really dealing with before you spend any money.

If you find a woman who interests you on a site that you don't want to work with and if you have her full name or other reasonably unique information or profile content, it is worth searching Google to see if she is listed on some other sites, better yet, on a free site. Many ladies post their profile on more than one site. This is a good method for excluding greedy agencies or those who refuse to part with direct contact information.

Irrespective of your contact method, you must decide what you are prepared to spend and how much hassle you are willing to endure. You can go the free, much-hassle route or you can go the expensive, hand-held route. Most men strike a medium somewhere in between, but you must find your own comfort level with this. Only work with agencies that you

How to Select an Agency or Contact Method

have verified to be reputable and who you can exclude from your communication at an early stage in the event that you choose to.

Be aware that, if you use some agency e-mail systems, they are often pre-programmed to strip out any attempt at communicating contact information to each other. Phone numbers, e-mail addresses and physical addresses are often censored this way. Of course, you are then locked into paying for each e-mail and that is exactly how some agencies want to keep it. Naturally they claim to be *protecting the women* by doing this but anybody can get a free disposable e-mail address so that doesn't really hold water. Again, it's all about the money.

The point to remember is that others are not cheap to feed. A greedy agency playing *piggy in the middle* will seldom be an asset to you. A good, reasonably priced agency who will work with you and butt out when required, may well be an asset to you.

To conclude this chapter, IMBRA is a subject that should be briefly covered for the benefit of Americans. If you are not American you can skip to the next chapter because you are not subject to its provisions.

January 5, 2006, was a day America took a big step towards an Orwellian society. It was when George Bush signed the International Marriage Broker Regulation Act, known as IMBRA. This law makes it illegal for Americans to meet foreign women via websites that specialize in such introductions, without first submitting to criminal background checks and having the foreign woman sign an approval that contact is allowed. This law is supposedly to save foreign women from abuse at the hands of American men.

Most people feel that IMBRA only displaces the problem it is aimed at and that it does not solve it. What it does do is inconvenience agencies and clients who do not want to be over regulated. So I better tell you the bare bones of it anyway so you know.

The IMBRA law is only applicable to US citizens and residents, and is only enforceable against US-registered agencies. A US citizen who uses a non-US agency that is not obligated to enforce US IMBRA laws (or as some Americans do, get a foreign friend to purchase the information for them) will have circumvented the law in the first instance.

The US touts the denial of a K1 fiancée visa and various other sanctions as punishment for the non-compliant citizen. However, if the US citizen claims to have met the woman while walking down the street or while feeding the ducks in the park, IMBRA would be effectively null and void as they had not met through an agency. Such a strategy is becoming the avenue of choice for US citizens who believe that their government should not interfere in their personal relationships.

If you are a government-fearing American, then you should find an Agency who is IMBRA compliant and fill out the required forms before exchanging contact information. If you use an agency who is not IMBRA compliant, your choices are either to be creative during the visa application process (which, of course, your author does not recommend) or to marry her abroad and go straight for the K3 spousal visa application, which is seemingly exempt, as yet. If you want a hassle-free K1 fiancée visa application and you want to be honest in your actions, talk to your agency to make sure you are covered if you are unsure. Even non-US agencies that do not routinely enforce IMBRA will do so rather than to lose a client.

How to Select an Agency or Contact Method

Certain methods of meeting women seem to be exempt from IMBRA. These would include introductions by mutual friends, introductions effected via free sites, chat programs (such as ICQ and Yahoo) and women who you happened upon while strolling casually down the street in *Dumpsk* while admiring the grey concrete Soviet apartments. It is claimed that if you currently meet by one of those methods that would remove you from the onerous confines of the IMBRA regulations.

You should expect that the US government will continue to tweak the laws to exclude popular escape avenues. Therefore, always double check the current position on the official sites and forums, if in doubt. If you are not an American, and you are still reading because you are nosy; thank your lucky stars you live in a free country that has resisted the temptation to exert such Orwellian control over its citizens' personal relationships.

Chapter Seven
Choosing Women to Contact

Online profiles can often be an admirable work of literary fiction. Many are written or content-assisted by agencies or friends of the women. They will do and say that which they think is necessary to attain the goal, just as many men in this pursuit do the same.

Naturally in the marketing environment that online dating is, it is thought better to present the positive information, or the information that it is believed that men are looking for. For this reason you will note many profiles all say pretty similar stuff. It seems every woman wants to *make cozy home*, loves nature, does sport, never smokes or drinks and is a general paragon of virtue earnestly waiting for her foreign swain to hop on a plane and whisk her away to his castle in the West.

While occasionally this may be true, you would be correct to be suspicious to note when perusing women's online profiles that most claim not to smoke or drink. This is not always true. It is true that modern Russian women are increasingly paying attention to good health, and healthcare must be usually paid for if it is to be of a decent standard. Cigarettes and alcohol cost money of course, and if one is on a budget then these may not be priority items. However, I have been in the company of Russian women, smoking a cigarette, who while doing so have earnestly explained that they do not really smoke.

The reality is that many women will drink and smoke, although in my experience it seems to be less black and white than in the West. Many

Choosing Women to Contact

women smoke very lightly and if a man seems particularly against it, she will claim not to smoke and will probably just give it up quietly, you may never know. Similarly with drinking, many women when single or with casual boyfriends will be often drunk as a skunk, but they know also that beer and wine has many calories and excessive calorie intake equals extra weight, which foreign men don't want. So the woman who claims not to drink or drinks only seldom, probably will stick to that when she meets her future husband.

Similarly with age gaps, many women will write they want to meet a man "up to forty" and many agencies will edit that to read "up to fifty-five" in order to make her more marketable and thus more profitable for them. Take profile information only as a rough guide, use later communication, conversation and face time to establish the real truth about the accuracy of her profile content.

You need to do some research on which cities you might want to visit before you even start writing. Find your potential cities by looking for a city with agencies you like the look of or women that you are considering writing to. Consider where you can reasonably get to also as mentioned already.

This is the problem with many of the large multi-agency conglomerates and affiliates, men will just jump right in and start writing to women from six different cities in four different countries, having given no consideration that these women may be thousands of miles apart. That will be a logistical nightmare when you come to get on a plane to meet a couple of them. If you have narrowed your agency list down to a handful, you will have a few possible regions to concentrate your search in.

As a broad rule of thumb, there are more available women in poorer parts of the FSU and less in the more affluent parts. Quality of life in Moscow, St Petersburg and the Baltic EU states of Estonia and Latvia for example, is nowadays rather good for many. Thus the desire to relocate abroad is less evident in the populous. Conversely, the quality of life in much of Ukraine, Belarus, Central Russia, Armenia and most of the "Stans" is lower, so there are more women in these places considering relocation.

In my opinion, Ukraine, and especially Kiev and Odessa, is now akin to an over-fished pond. Ukraine has been awash with bride hunting Americans - and others who can now travel visa free to Ukraine - for many years. Many of these men are merely masquerading as bride-seekers but in fact are merely sex tourists. Many of the local women have become jaded to these sex tourists promising the earth and delivering nothing, and as such, some Ukrainian cities have attracted the undesirable element. There are many scammers, prostitutes and professional daters seeking only to empty your pocket in the shops and restaurants.

The Ukrainian dating scene has become known to some as "the dirty barrel." Many dubious local men have become arrangers, interpreters and guides, for a Western price of course. I am not suggesting you won't find good people there to help you, or some genuine women, but I believe your odds for success are reduced there. If you want to go to Ukraine, consider looking outside of Kiev and Odessa my sources tell me.

Bride seekers have a better chance in Russia I believe. I always advise people to avoid Moscow and St Petersburg for the reasons mentioned already, in addition to which, these are not cheap places to stay or entertain ladies. Central Moscow prices are comparable to London or New York prices. These places are for tourists. Many serious bride seekers also avoid the very poor areas of Russia to reduce the chance of encountering a woman who only wants to marry a passport or a *Green Card Girl* (as Americans call them). Many men report success in finding women from mid-sized Russian towns and cities, towns that are neither poor nor particularly rich. Examples would include Samara, Togliatti, Ufa, Chelyabinsk, Kazan, Saratov, Tver, etc.

Do some research on the towns the women you have seen live in, in fact do some general geographical research on any potential target country or region. Meeting a woman in the Siberian wilderness may seem attractive until you find she is six hours by train from the nearest provincial airport, and the train sometimes doesn't run.

Think ahead. Yes, of course meeting her in a mutually agreeable and more accessible third town will be a possibility the first time, but at some stage you need to meet the parents, so you are going to her town. If you marry her she will occasionally want to visit her hometown and maybe it costs thousands to get there if it is remote, make sure you consider these things at the outset.

You may decide to search in Kazakhstan, Belarus, Armenia or Moldova or another part of the FSU. Every place is different. Turkmenistan for example is known to be quite hostile to Westerners. I would avoid Chechnya also; it was recently a war zone. But we are all different, some men would relish the places I might avoid. I recently met a Canadian man in England en route to Georgia, who had connecting flights through my city. We had lunch. Georgia is certainly a lesser-trod path for bride seekers, but he believes he has found his woman there and is now engaged and living there on a part time basis.

The FSU and Eastern European countries that are now EU such as Lithuania, Latvia, Estonia, Poland, Czech Republic, Romania and Bulgaria have their fair share of ethnic Russians. EU passport holders have no difficulty moving to another part of the EU and less difficulty moving to the US, Australia, or elsewhere. You should not exclude these countries from your search. There are fewer women willing to relocate from these places due to the relative prosperity there. You will find some, and you are only looking for one aren't you?

A lady with an EU passport is a boon for any European as she can probably relocate with the minimum of fuss and bureaucracy and you will avoid the expensive visa procedure and associated financial scrutiny if you are European yourself. Perhaps you would consider relocating? I can tell you from first hand experience that Estonia and Poland are excellent places to live. With some research, you will find the target area you feel comfortable about. Sometimes you will find the woman who is your first choice, and target your initial search around her area.

Having found a reputable agency or two, and some potential women in agreeable locations, you are ready to peruse the profiles with a more serious attitude. When looking through the profiles, check all the points, both positive and negative. Do not give into temptation of writing to somebody who is not what you are looking for and do not be swayed only by photographs. Remember, you are possibly going to live with this person for the rest of your life, and beauty is only skin deep. Try to look beyond agency photographs.

Choosing Women to Contact

Many Russian women have small model type portfolios of themselves; this is popular and inexpensive to do in Russia. These are the pictures that a woman will often use in her agency profile; she may look quite different in everyday life. Also, often these photographs may be a few years old, another reason to look beyond agency front page photographs of the nineteen-year-old über babes mentioned earlier. Sometimes it is nicer to see a woman who has put natural everyday photographs on her profile. However, women when they do this usually use the photographs *they like* which are often quite different to what we are looking for. Her holiday photograph taken in Greece, now on her bedside table, that gives her fond memories, and that her mother thinks is lovely, looks to us like some tourist girl you would not look twice at, sweltering at ninety degrees in day-glo flip flops.

Check all the pictures she has put online; you will be asking for more later on of course. Many men when browsing websites do not look at all the available photographs of the lady. Do not make that mistake. I passed over my own (now) wife's thumbnail a few times before taking a closer look because the first picture didn't catch my eye. The second was not much better, yet the third one made me look closer. She looked like a different woman in each of them. So much so, that the agency hosting her profile, in her town, had a service where you could pay a modest price for twenty-five photographs they took in their office, if the woman agreed. I did this - even though she argued about it - and I was very pleasantly surprised by the results. We met the following month. My wife still thinks those original photographs she submitted are wonderful, yet they almost made me skip over her profile.

Do not be shy about copying pictures that pique your interest to your computer and blowing them up for closer inspection. This may be the future mother of your children. Pay more attention to genetics and bone structure than the awful Russian fringe or bad dye job she may be sporting. Cosmetic things can be changed later; hair can grow and change color easily. If you don't like her hooker boots, you can buy her some new ones later if you have any money left. She will be looking at your photographs in a similar manner.

You are now operating outside of the normal parameters you are used to when looking for women in your country. You can chat to local women often for the price of a polite greeting and a glass of wine. Having that same glass of wine with a Russian woman will involve a plane journey and many other associated expenses. You are correct to be choosy; do not feel guilty about this.

The whole of Russia and its surrounding FSU area, together comprising a sixth of the world's land mass, are your oyster from which you must extract your pearl. Take your time. Stay realistic. If you live in a small town, stay away from girls from big cities and capitals (Moscow, St. Petersburg, Kiev, Odessa, Minsk, etc.). Women from such cities will likely struggle to adapt to a life in a small town. Likewise, if you live in London or New York, think carefully before contacting a village girl. You should by now be considering your future wife's later adaptation. You will be taking her not only to another culture and country, but to another type of living she may not be comfortable with. You should consider this at the beginning of your search. If you are unfamiliar with her town and its size consult Wikipedia on the internet for up to date information on her city.

Choosing Women to Contact

That said, many village girls dream of living in a big city. Many Russian girls aspire to live in Moscow; it is the Holy Grail to them. If you find one of these village girls, your coming from a large foreign city would present no problem.

If you are from a small town, she may initially recoil in horror. Western small towns are very different to FSU small towns. The majority of Russian ladies tend to be rather cosmopolitan. The reason is that in Russia, living in a small town or village often is a nightmare. There can be very grim conditions, no entertainment, no goods to buy; even TV reception may not be available. Russian ladies do not know or understand the difference between small towns in Russia and abroad, and they have this instinctive fear of small towns. She will imagine you don't have running water and have to suffer a sporadic electricity supply.

Since small towns are often not attractive places in the FSU, you must back up your disclosure that you live in a small town with its qualifications. Mention the local shopping mall, theatres, restaurants and other relevant things that are within easy reach. Mention why you enjoy living there. Do mention how far the nearest decent size town is. A Russian woman sometimes imagines life in a foreign small town akin to living in a prison. She will imagine not being able to go out, no buses, shops or civilization within easy reach. Educate her in this regard before she asks; discuss in detail your hometown in your introduction letter.

The next issue you must consider is the woman's knowledge of English. At some point in your search, you will have to decide for yourself how much English a lady must know in order for you to form a lasting relationship. You must find your own comfort level with this subject. The forthcoming language chapter covers this in much more detail.

Of course, a woman who meets a man she considers potential marriage material will quickly busy herself in learning English by whatever means available to her, if she hasn't started already. Having established she is serious and genuine, a gift of a good dictionary and maybe an electronic translator will help immensely. The language issue can be an indicator of intellectual curiosity; an alarm bell should ring in your head if the woman is well into a correspondence with you and still not attempting to learn to communicate in English, especially after the first meeting.

Before her search for a foreign man, she should have realized she needed to learn his language; usually that language will be English. Sometimes a woman who is looking to Europe will hold off on language lessons in case she needs to learn Dutch, Danish, German or French instead. But having entered into a serious communication, she should be making some progress if you are going to consider her intent seriously.

I know a man who spent several years searching for non-English speaking women. His favored English development technique was to buy two identical copies of a Russian dictionary/phrasebook and mail one copy to the woman. During daily telephone conversations, they read the phrases which have a Russian translation together. In conversation, if she got stuck on a word, they could check it. Since they used identical books, the time spent searching for a phrase or for a dictionary entry was greatly reduced by him indicating the page number. The only prerequisite is a familiarity with English numbers and the English alphabet.

Unlike internet communication, time spent in this manner will be productive preparation for a visit. In any case, immersion is a very effective language builder. The same situation holds true for a man who is involved in a relationship with a Russian speaker. For those who are not mentally lazy, learning some Russian is not such a daunting challenge as you might imagine. You will end up teaching each other language.

If you choose to target women with limited English, your task will indeed be harder, but there is the possibility you will be meeting a woman many other men chose not to contact. Accept that at least on your first visit to such a woman you may have to be accompanied by an interpreter. While this does quell the flames of a developing romance somewhat, it is not an insurmountable barrier to many men. Some consider it an interesting challenge. I know many men who have married women who couldn't speak ten words of English at first contact, but they are all fluent now. I also know men who married their interpreter, but that's another story. You must decide early on what minimum level of English you can accept at the beginning, and go from there.

Some agencies allow you to see how many times a woman has had her contact details purchased or when she last exchanged a letter through the agency. (And some lie about it.) A man would be foolish to write to a woman whose contact information has been sold two hundred times. Such a woman has the luxury of being extremely selective and the value of new men contacting her decreases. This scenario is advantageous for the woman but very disadvantageous for the unfortunate men who write to her. If a man writes to many women who are less heavily-pursued, the dynamics of the situation are reversed. Now the man has the luxury of being more selective and his perceived value to the women increases.

When reading profiles you will see many women list under "professions or occupations" that they are psychologists, economists, doctors, lawyers, teachers and many other professional sounding titles. Many sport several degrees. However, the education required to obtain these qualifications is different than required in the West and often people don't work in the area they obtained degrees in.

In Russia people go where the money is and it is frequently not in professional occupations, especially government funded ones. It is not unusual to find a qualified doctor working as an office manager, a psychologist working in a kindergarten or a shop girl with three degrees in something obscure. Don't rely too much on profession or occupation as a snap indicator of intelligence; you must use communication to make this judgment.

Professions and occupations are never what they seem and rarely correlate with income. Under the communist system when all people were allegedly financially equal, the only indicator of status became education. That thinking has remained, and this is one reason why most people go to a university. The corruption of past eras has also remained however, and this still allows people to pay a bribe to get good marks and eventually degrees.

By now you should have a pretty good idea what type of woman you are looking for, where she may be from and the level of English she must have. You will have started to give consideration to some of the fundamental issues that elude many people until much later. At this early stage you are now relatively well informed and prepared for the next step. Only now are you ready to flash the credit card at an agency or two and contact some women.

Chapter Eight
Making Progress - Communication

Depending on the agency or method you use, you may get full contact information straight away, or you may just get a postal address or an e-mail address. Your early objective is to make sure you have her full name, address, phone numbers, e-mail address and anything else you can get as soon as you can politely and reasonably obtain them. So contact her first by e-mail, letter or via the agency if you must. You need to do your scam checks as mentioned earlier before you get too involved. If you have her number, do not call her out of the blue.

I suggest contacting two or three women at a time; more than five and you will get confused. Even with two or three, keep notes. You don't want to ask Svetlana how her job in the lawyers' office is going when Svetlana actually works in the kindergarten. It is easily done.

You should first know what a "Keyboard Romeo" is. As the name suggests, a Keyboard Romeo is the bane of this endeavor to the women. He will write and write all kinds of sweet nothings, string her on for months and months on end, when finally pressed for a visit, he will disappear, and move on to the next fantasy girl he wants many photographs from and never intends to visit. It is very important from the outset that you are not perceived as a Keyboard Romeo, lest you be dropped like a hot potato. In addition, it is important to be honest with the women to whom you are writing.

It is acceptable to send the same introduction letter to all women, not forgetting to change her name obviously, but you will have much better results if the letter is custom made to fit her profile a little. You need to write about one or two pages about yourself, your life, what you like and dislike, the place you live, your work, your education, and whether you have been married previously and, if not, why not? (Tip: Because you were first busy with your studies/career, and by the time you had established yourself, you could not find the right woman - most were already married).

Do *not* write at length about your divorce or its reasons and do *not* complain about overweight, feminist Western women and what you dislike about them. Do give her a credible reason why you decided to look for a wife in Russia and why you liked her profile in a polite way. She knows already she is pretty, so be more creative than that. If there are some important things on your personal checklist that are not reflected in her profile, ask her about them.

Do *not* talk about any sexual subjects or anything that can be interpreted as such. Talking about sex in early stages of correspondence with Russian women is a definite turn off. You will be able to discuss it later when you know each other much better but not yet. In general, Russian women enjoy sex, as do all women, but they find it inappropriate to talk about it with people they hardly know.

If you are planning to visit her country soon, or if you are ready to visit her country as soon as you find the woman you are looking for, tell her about it. She knows about Keyboard Romeo's remember and will be watching for them. At the end of your letter, tell her that you are waiting for her response and want her to answer in any event, even if she is not

Making Progress - Communication

interested, just to let you know. Tell her that you will accept her decision, whatever it will be, and will not bother her again if she does not find you interesting, but you would like to know that she received and read your letter anyway. (You won't believe how many more responses this short phrase will produce; it shows that you are really interested in her!)

Paragraph breaks in your letter are absolutely essential. There is nothing worse than wading through an unbroken lump of text. Don't do it! The most important thing to bear in mind is that your letter should stand out from the rest. Remember, whomever you write to is almost certainly getting other letters, maybe dozens of them, from other guys. Why should she pick you? Keep asking yourself that question because it will do more than anything else to keep you focused and motivated on getting the results you want. Never forget, you are selling yourself. This is marketing. Unless the *goods* (you) are appealing and attractive, *shoppers* (the women) will simply pass you by.

Include at the bottom your postal and e-mail addresses and phone and fax numbers in international format. (Example: +44 123 456 7890 for the UK, +1 123 555 6789 for the US.) Don't worry; she will not pop up at your door tomorrow, but you might receive a surprise call or SMS from her when you least expect it. Print your letter on your computer if writing by snail mail. Russian women consider handwritten letters cheap; also they are much more difficult to read.

I highly recommend you have your introductory letter professionally translated into Russian irrespective of her claimed English ability. Do *not* use translation software for this. Even if a woman claims good English, she will not be able to enjoy it as much if her English is not perfect. When reading a well-translated letter in her own language, she can enjoy it and she will be very grateful you made the effort to make it easier for her. Many men are too cheap to do that small thing and you may be ignored if she thinks your software translation makes you look greedy. (There's that word again!) Enclose a copy of your letter in English also, so that she may read both together later on; the English one will help her language skills too. What a considerate chap you are! You will also be able to express yourself fully and your great sense of humor if you use a professional translator.

Here is an example as to why to avoid machine translations. I just typed into the best online translator I know the phrase: *"I was very interested when I read your profile; some of your interests are very similar to mine. I would be very interested in the possibility of getting to know you."* I machine translated it into Russian, then back to English and this is what I got: *"I very much was interested, when I read your structure; some of your interests are very similar to mine. I very much would be interested in an opportunity uznavanija you."* Whilst you may be able to get the gist of the translated sentence, it is not the stuff deep meaningful communication is made from. (For what its worth, the word "uznavanija,"(узнавания) while not a technically correct Russian word, is recognized by my wife as the machine's attempt to produce a similar word that means "to recognize." That improves the translated attempt not one bit.) Use machine translation only for short unimportant letters with women you are also in telephone contact with. Play with the software a little over time and you will learn how to phrase sentences in such a way as they make better sense, but do not rely on it for anything serious.

You can either make a template letter for all ladies (which is cheaper), or make one template and add separate paragraphs for each lady designed specially for her, and also have those translated, which is a bit more expensive but produces much better results. If you use the right person to translate your letter, each woman will compliment you on what you have written and thank you for taking the trouble to translate it to her language. It will show her you are considerate and you are already ahead of the competition. If you still insist on sending your letter only in English, write it in simple words and phrases so she can understand; avoid euphemisms, slang and incorrect spelling. Many women can read uncomplicated English, since most Russians study English at school.

Finally, make it clear that you are a *serious man*. You are not a Keyboard Romeo, a sex tourist or a time waster are you? You must get that point subtly across. Many of the women you are writing to have been led up the garden path by other foreign men in the past or may have been dumped or otherwise abused by them. You must demonstrate you are not like that. I would suggest something like: *"I am totally serious about finding my future wife. I do not want to waste your time by only writing for many months. If we find we like each other and share similar interests and goals, I would want to visit you in your home city within the next few months."*

You *must* include your photographs with the first letter. A letter without photographs has an almost zero chance of receiving an answer. The photographs should ideally be professionally done, preferably in a suit and tie. Russian people like serious looking photographs for introductions. If you do not own a suit, at least wear a dress shirt for your pictures. A good photographer will be able to make you look attractive even if you are not exactly the most handsome of chaps. If you have a great body, include also a photograph in a muscle hugging T-shirt. Never send photographs in sloppy beach shorts or without a shirt, it is rather disrespectful.

The best introduction letter in the world is useless without decent photographs. In this instance, as with many things in life, pictures really are worth a thousand words. Make sure at least one photograph is full face and shows your eyes. Russian women like to see your eyes as they are the window to your soul. Just as importantly, all your photographs should be recent. None should show your new Mustang GT, motorbike, boat, house, swimming pool, or worst of all, the severed arm of an ex-girlfriend or wife around your neck. Ideally send about three or four photographs. The photographs should all be different, meaning different clothes and backgrounds. Three-quarter body shots with nice big smiles also get good results. Good photographs are often ones of you standing in your garden, or perhaps with a background of a lake or leafy spot; nature shots are popular.

If sending a letter by snail mail, obtaining complete contact information is paramount as soon as possible. Mail from the West to the FSU can often take up to a month or more and who wants to wait that long every time? If you only have her mailing address, ask in the introduction letter that she allows you to have her e-mail address (if she has one) or other contact info by return if she is interested in communicating with you. A sneaky one is to ask her to SMS you when she received your letter "just so you know." Then you have her mobile number already without asking. Have your interpreter call her to get the rest of her contact information while arranging a three-way call maybe, that way you have hit the ground running.

Making Progress - Communication

If you get no reply to your introduction letter, don't worry about it. If you sent your letter via an agency ask them about it. The better ones will call her and chase it up. If you used direct e-mail, send another message after maybe a week, include a copy of the original, and politely ask if she received the first one. If you receive no reply, take her off your list.

Hopefully fairly soon you will have a reply from one or two ladies, perhaps with a mobile number and more contact information. You might send her an SMS telling her you received her letter and that you will reply soon. Even if she has zero English, she will have a friend who will translate an SMS, and after all it's about time she learned some isn't it? The development of the relationship at this stage should be little different from any other developing relationship with a local woman. There is one difference though; you must remember you are wife-hunting. You need to know fundamental things early on, not after six or eight months, so basically you must learn to converse in reverse.

To converse in reverse basically means you need to address serious matters early in the correspondence because of the distance, trouble and expense involved. Certainly, after the first meeting all-important issues should have been covered to some degree. Then during subsequent trips and communication you do what normally you would do first - get to know her better. You need to know very early on if this woman is potential wife material. This must be done in a subtle way though. You must mingle these questions in one by one rather than rapid fire them at her in a demanding way. She does not want to feel she is interviewing for a job, which in many ways she actually is, but you must keep that fact hidden behind genuine romantic posturing, because you are a gentleman aren't you?

You need to sound her out on children issues first and foremost; does she want any, or any more? Do you? Her feelings about your children if you have any, and the role they play in your life, must be discussed. The children issue will be a big deal to most women, so you must not ignore this issue. You must cover religious issues, attitudes to life and work, her future ambitions and dreams. Make sure she would be comfortable in the environment where you live. In writing, try to ask open questions designed to elicit detailed responses, questions that require explanation rather than "yes" or "no" replies.

Europe and most of the world can SMS (text message) the FSU directly just by using the international format, for example Russia is +7 XXX, Ukraine is +38 XXX. This is not always possible from the US. Americans must check with their cell provider and ask. If not, you can find a web based SMS service that you can use, often free. Start with the website of her FSU service provider; often you can do it from there. Find out from her who it is and tag a ".ru" on the end and you will find their website most likely. You will find resources on our website to help you with this.

It does not take very long to get a nice communication by e-mail and SMS going, and it shouldn't take very long to decide if she is a serious potential wife candidate and if you are one for her also. If it doesn't feel right, it isn't right. Trust your gut feelings; move on to the next one if your gut says no. Don't waste time and build her or your hopes up falsely. If you need to dump a correspondent, don't just go silent on her; she may worry about you and wonder if you are okay. Be a gentleman about it;

Making Progress - Communication

send her a short e-mail or letter and politely let her know that you don't think that you have a potential future together. Thank her for her time and let her know how nice it was to have met her and wish her good luck in all her endeavors in the future. She should at least then respect you for having the courtesy to be honest with her. Conversely, women do not always do the same; if a woman goes quiet on you, nudge her a few times by e-mail and SMS and then leave it. If two weeks passes, consider yourself dumped.

Not everyone in the FSU has a computer at home. Those that do are often on old fashioned dial-up internet and they pay for it by buying scratch cards from kiosks which gives a length of time or amount of traffic for a fixed price. (So don't send her twenty 700KB pictures or video files!) Personal text based instant message programs such as Windows Messenger, MSN, Yahoo and Google Talk are becoming popular also. Ask her if she has such a program. Fast broadband internet connections are still in their infancy in the FSU; bigger cities are served easier and more cheaply. If you find a woman who has one, introduce her quickly to VOIP for free PC to PC calls between you both with a program such as Skype. Sometimes a woman will have access to a work PC with a fast connection.

You have struck gold if you find a woman who has a fast home connection; it will save you a fortune in calls and you can do webcam chats too, but don't expect to find too many women with such technology in the FSU just yet. Nowadays the service is available but the $40 a month it costs is often prohibitive for many.

Google has an instant message chat program too called Google Talk, which has a built in translator. If you want to try it, just add *en2ru@bot.talk.google.com* as a friend in Google Talk and send it a message to translate from English to Russian. (It works the same in reverse with the address *ru2en@bot.talk.google.com*) You can use it as an interpreter in your chat or as a pocket translator in your Google Talk client for your Blackberry. Again, don't rely on such services as a primary communication technique; just have fun with them. On our resources website detailed at the end of the book you will find more information and links to this service.

Sometimes you will find a woman who is unfamiliar with the internet, does not have a computer and thus no e-mail address. This can be problematic, but not insurmountable. If pressed a little, she can no doubt find an inexpensive internet café or a friend's computer to use and have a friend give her a crash course on how to set up and use a free e-mail account. If she has limited or no access to the internet, you must increase the frequency of your forthcoming telephone communication straight away.

The next milestone after you have developed a rapport over a week or two by one means or another is to move on to the telephone conversations. If a woman, even from the poorest grey concrete backwater of the FSU, tells you she has no mobile telephone (cell phone), she is almost certainly lying as mentioned in the scams chapter. Russian women almost all have a mobile telephone, it is a major fashion accessory, and probably she will have the latest camera phone more exclusive than yours!

Russian women are often to be seen walking down the street talking loudly into phones. It is a consumer exhibitionism thing in Russia, and it

Making Progress - Communication

goes hand in hand with the expensive designer sunglasses she will also own. Seldom is a Russian woman without an up to date mobile telephone and the latest diamante encrusted designer sunglasses. She will buy these things before food quite often. (Now you know why she is slim!)

If you encounter a woman who insists she doesn't have a phone, be *very* cautious. It is quite conceivable that she won't have a phone at home as there is sometimes an installation waiting list and a bribe to pay to get it connected (another reason she *will* have a mobile telephone), but there will be one at her neighbors, parents, workplace, education establishment or friend's house that she can use to receive an incoming call. If she insists she has no access to a phone of any description, you must conclude you have met Hairy Boris again, or a woman who is not serious. It is time to move on. A woman who cannot make herself available for telephone communication has not thought through the implications of having a foreign swain. If you encounter this situation, a similar polite letter or e-mail as before should be used explaining that if she is unable to be contacted by telephone, then she is unable to maintain or develop an international relationship.

By now we shall assume you have e-mail contact and a telephone number or two for her. Do not call her out of the blue, without warning. She will be startled to be expected to hold an impromptu conversation in her second language that she seldom uses (assuming she speaks English at all), without mental preparation. If you do this, you can expect embarrassed giggling, startled silence or a hang up. No lady will want an unannounced international call when in the supermarket or on the bus.

Three-way calls with an interpreter in the middle are very useful and quite popular. Often the interpreter you find will be a relocated Russian wife of a foreign man herself, if you are lucky you will find an interpreter who was also a psychologist in Russia and who will be able to expertly advise you on how best to approach any situations you encounter. For instance, my wife was a psychology lecturer in Russia and has performed this service for dozens of men; a Russian female psychologist on your side can be an invaluable asset.

The interpreter usually initiates the call with you and then links your lady in on a three-way connection and you pay the interpreter a fixed price per hour or minute inclusive of call charges. This type of conversation can be a little impersonal however and should not be used as the exclusive means of communication. Use these calls maybe as a once a week tool as communication develops. Three-way calling with interpreters, while useful, does nothing to encourage her to learn English, something she must begin to do.

A good idea is for the interpreter to call the lady a day or two before, introduce herself, explain that she will be hosting the forthcoming three-way conversation, run the lady through what will happen, arrange a day and time and discuss with her any reservations she may have. This way you will often get, in advance, the interpreter's opinion of the lady following that native tongue conversation. This information alone can often be invaluable as it can be a source of confirmation of her sincerity, education and overall attitude and manner.

The necessity for a three-way call will of course depend entirely on the lady's English skills, but if she has zero English or is not too confident, three-way calls will be the way to start. Prior to a three-way, let the

Making Progress - Communication

interpreter call her for a moment or two before you are linked in, just to give her a moment of preparation. Following a three-way call, hang up and let the interpreter have a few minutes conversation with the lady to ascertain how much (if any) she understood of your English and her impression of you on the telephone. You can speak later with your interpreter to learn this most useful information.

Before you start any telephone calls, familiarize yourself with the time zone she is in. The Russian Federation and the FSU is a vast area spanning eleven time zones from GMT+2 to GMT+12, so check the time zone for her city. Having done that, get yourself a long distance telephone service provider or phone card. You can call the FSU for peanuts from most countries if you do some research first. You may also need to use this to set up your three-way call. You will find resources on our website to help you with this.

Make a plan with her when you will call her, even if she has minimal English and is shy about it, "just to hear your voice" should swing it. Your first call is really to touch base; it doesn't have to be too involved and can be quite short. Prepare her for the call by e-mail and SMS as mentioned already. Your second call a few days later will get longer and soon you will be talking like two old Babushkas (old women) over the garden fence before you know it. I cannot stress enough the importance of regular telephone calls if you want to build a relationship. Four to seven times a week would be normal if you want to get anywhere. If her English is very poor or non-existent, you can consider using a three-way interpreter for later calls until her English becomes passable.

The man I referenced earlier who used the Russian dictionary/phrasebook technique also had a follow up procedure. He considers standard three-way calls quite impersonal. During telephone conversations, they read the phrases which have a Russian translation together. After each call he relayed by e-mail to his interpreter the general content together with anything he or she didn't understand. The interpreter would then call the girl and clarify the conversation content and help her with any phrases she did not understand. Although tedious and more expensive, this technique does have the benefit of spurring the woman into learning English by other additional means as she gained confidence in her developing language skills.

On the telephone, there are no hard and fixed rules. You and each woman must develop the method that works for you both best. Every situation is different and mostly dependant on her initial and developing English language level. When on the telephone, and especially in the early stages, slow your speech and make your pronunciation very distinct; avoid slang and euphemisms and stick to short simple sentences. Do not be afraid to test your Russian language on her either; the worst she can do is laugh and admire your effort.

Just because you are now speaking regularly on the phone do not abandon writing by e-mail or even snail mail. Provided that the lady has a decent command of English or at least developing English, there is everything to be gained by writing e-mails and letters as well as phoning and nothing to be lost.

Getting to know someone through correspondence requires a certain facility with language and the ability to express oneself without ambiguity or misapprehension. Writing has many advantages over the telephone. It

Making Progress - Communication

allows both parties the time to choose and compose their thoughts with care before sending them. Furthermore, many Russian women who have studied English at University are far better at reading and writing English than speaking it.

Assuming that you have both passed each others unspoken suitability tests by now, and are communicating nicely by e-mail and telephone, now is the time to demonstrate that you are not a Keyboard Romeo and make a plan to visit her. Because you are an organized sort of guy and a "serious man" you will have already used the resources on our website and other internet resources and be fully conversant with how you are going to get to her city and the likely cost. You will have a provisional month in mind which should be within the next three months. She won't sit around waiting for you forever, and she wants to know that you will meet her in person within a reasonable timeframe.

You must not convince yourself she is your "girlfriend" until you have actually met her in person. Before you meet in person she is merely your pen friend and telephone buddy; her life continues as before and she has merely made a little time for you in it. Until she actually is your girlfriend you have no rights over her movements and should not question her about her personal life in too much detail. She is unlikely to be sitting at home each evening sewing buttons on the local blind pensioners' apparel.

If you think these women are sitting at home on Friday and Saturday nights waiting for a foreign man's telephone call or e-mail, while gazing wistfully at a map of your country, you are not being too realistic. All young women (and men) have hormones and want friendship and companionship. Most women do have a local boyfriend but with many of them it is only a boyfriend of convenience, someone to go to the club with or to a café with other friends.

Many of these women after reaching their mid to late-twenties realize that they would prefer to marry a different type of man than what a lot of FSU men are. As such, many of these women remain serious in looking for a foreign husband while still having local boyfriends and when they find this good future foreign husband, it's "goodbye local boyfriend!"

Leave no stone unturned in your communication. This is real work; you must be able to commit the time and resources to this endeavor. If you only send a weekly e-mail and call every ten days, you are not serious, and she will know it. If you had a potential girlfriend in your hometown how often would you call her? I doubt it would be once a week. Use that as a guide to keep you focused on the goal of your endeavor.

The biggest obstacle to communication is language, so language is just what we will explore next.

Chapter Nine
Overcoming Language Barriers

A woman's knowledge of English will play a huge role in your developing relationship. There are two extremes – fluent English versus no English. You must ultimately decide where between the two extremes you are comfortable.

One point of view is that lack of communication is the number one cause of failure in all relationships. If you can't talk to each other, then how do you know you are truly compatible? Do not underestimate the language barrier. How can you know a person without a common language?

Language barriers are why many relationships tend to fail. It is not because of age differences or cultural disparities, but simply the inability to communicate at a meaningful level that causes problems. Communication is the greatest single hurdle to building a relationship. Getting to know a woman is hard enough when you both speak and comprehend the same language; doing it when one or other can only communicate via a translator is asking for trouble.

She can learn English, of course, but while she's still in Russia it's going to take a long time even studying English at a university. After her relocation, assimilation will make the process much quicker, but by then it may be too late, because she is already in your country. By the time she learns acceptable English and is able to converse at real, natural flowing conversation speed, who knows? You just might find she is not the same lady you thought you knew and ultimately married.

When I was searching, I specifically targeted women who had a basic grasp of oral and written English. My wife had an English level accurately described as "I can translate a letter with a dictionary, though it may take a few hours. I can talk with you in limited English if you speak slowly and distinctly." Only after a lot of lessons, telephone calls, hard work and spending a lot of time visiting the UK did her English reach an acceptable standard that one could actually operate a relationship with.

Many agencies overstate a woman's English level. Most allow the woman to describe her ability without testing it. Beware of a woman who is shy to move on to telephone conversations because her English level is artificially boosted by the agency or software translation. Agency letters are frequently a giveaway, as they often feature the same well-worn phrases like "making a cozy home," "love to cook tasty meals" and the old favorite "I am looking for *the* serious man." I treated all women with stuff that like in their early correspondence with a bit of caution, at least until a few letters had been exchanged, and I was able to move onto telephone calls to directly ascertain her true English level.

The opposite point of view suggests that low or zero English women are worth considering. The women who are more or less fluent - or at least have a basic grasp of English - represent a relatively small percentage of the total women available. If your original objective is to increase the size of your dating pool, you may shoot yourself in the foot by discounting those who speak little or no English.

Some people argue you don't have to have perfect communication initially, and that the lack of communication is not an insurmountable ob-

Overcoming Language Barriers

stacle. If a man and a woman can sit down and struggle through communicating simple ideas to each other over a dictionary, there would have to be a tremendous amount of dedication on the part of both of them. Some claim that this is more meaningful than two people who meet and spend a few hours fluently talking about art, politics or whatever their mutual interests are.

When you are together 24/7 with no interpreter, then how can you interact if you can't understand each other? The answer is that you just can't do it. She must learn English without exception, so how will this happen during your communication and visiting period? Unless you are prepared to pay for some English lessons for your lady, you are better served in concentrating on women with at least some English speaking ability.

When you believe you may have found "the one," and preferably after you have met her, it is time to invest in some English lessons for your lady, regardless of her English level (unless she is fluent). Lessons arranged by her agency are generally to be avoided. Insincere women have been known not to attend the agency lessons the hapless man abroad is paying for. Instead the girl and the agency split the money and report to you on her slow progress. You want none of that behavior, or even the temptation to engage in it. She knows her area better than you. She knows what will work best if you quiz her a little. She will be able to find a private English tutor. See what she suggests and use your better judgment.

Do not be surprised if she tries to refuse money for these lessons or offers to pay for them herself. She quite likely can't afford to pay herself, but does not want to be seen to be accepting money from you. You will encounter this attitude with many respectable FSU women with various things you will need to pay for; how you overcome it differs as to her character. Find a way to make her accept it; call it a gift or an investment in the future. Explain that as "her man" you have decided already and it is not negotiable. If you know her, as you should by now, you will find a way to overcome the Russian woman pride issue with money.

Some of these women will think it's strange for you to pay for her lessons; it's not natural to them. Since the way you became acquainted is not entirely natural in their eyes, they may see this as an attempt to have some good old-fashioned economic advantage over them. Some men think that way and women know this.

Many women we have worked with have expressed surprise that some guy on the other side of the world is prepared to fund English lessons for them and sometimes an internet connection to facilitate communication and language development. Funding such things from afar remains the best way to allow a genuine woman to make significant progress. I will insert the caveat again, however: Only fund anything of this nature with a woman you have spoken with often and validated beyond any shadow of a doubt.

Attending a school or college may not be workable as she probably works full time and can't attend daytime classes. The favored method is private tutors. Every woman knows someone who is fluent; many will know, or know of, English teachers already who will probably teach in the local university or college. These are the best people for your woman to have as a private tutor. Professionals in the FSU do not receive large salaries. Many of them work as private tutors after hours to supplement their

Overcoming Language Barriers

income. Well-qualified teachers can be found this way at very reasonable prices. My wife used to get private tuition this way from a pensioner called *Vladislav* in Russia. Budget up to $10 an hour allowing for some inflation and city variation. Perhaps more in larger and capital cities.

Even a couple of hours of good tutoring a week will soon be noticeable. English lessons in conjunction with your daily telephone conversations, a few English books, a good dictionary, your SMS messages and e-mails she must now translate and respond to, will create a radical improvement in her skill level. Your aim is to immerse her from a distance in simple but daily and persistent English.

Hopefully she will soon become very motivated as she makes progress, and next time you visit, the gift of some simple English books, maybe children's easy reading books, will help her construction no end. It might be a long and slow battle but after a few months you can be holding an elementary conversation with a woman whose English was formerly near zero. Assuming your woman started with a reasonable level of English, she will be moving ever closer toward being fluent.

Your goal must be that your lady speaks English sufficient to converse at a basic level before she comes to your country. After that you can get her into a local educational establishment in your own country if needed or rely on assimilation and adaptation thereafter.

Often times, as a matter of pride, your lady will want to speak flawless English as soon a possible after her arrival in your country. Be prepared to help her attain this goal. Your relationship's future will be much more solid.

Most important is you both together get to a level by whatever means of being able to communicate adequately with each other. Yes I said *both* of you; do you think the onus should be *all* on her? Read on!

You may meet a woman who is Ukrainian, Latvian or Estonian. Some of these women will argue that *their* language is their first language, not Russian. In some cases that will be true; in many cases she will know her language *and* Russian already being of Russian heritage. Ukrainian is very similar to Russian anyway (although some Ukrainian women may argue about that). Estonian is closer to Finnish. Latvian is closer to old Germanic European and Baltic languages. Those who are satellite state descended, born and bred may argue that they don't speak Russian, will not, have never, and don't want to.

If you meet a woman who genuinely does not speak Russian, you may have to look into her language. That said, most FSU non-Russian speaking women will speak English, because in the real world you need Russian or English in their part of the world to get by. Local dialects only will not cut it unless she has never left her small village. However, virtually all of the women we talk of here will speak Russian. This leads me nicely to my next suggestion.

You should learn some Russian. That is not as horrid an idea as it may sound and you don't need to have a high IQ to do so. At some stage you will need or want to learn at least *some* Russian, so you may as well make a start now.

Learning some Russian language will put you far ahead of most other men in your quest. Imagine the fun you can have knowing some Russian. Imagine being able to sit with your lady in a restaurant in your country and freely discuss the other diners? (Within earshot but not understood!)

Overcoming Language Barriers

Maybe at a family gathering you just want to blurt out the odd phrase or sentence or maybe just, "Darling, don't discuss that topic please" or something similar.

She will have to learn English or your language primarily, but should the entire onus be on her? Consider when you are in Russia, if you need to go to a drug store; you need to know what the word looks like don't you? There is not one single reason why you shouldn't learn some, but hundreds of reasons why you should. You need not be fluent at all; simply the basic grasp of a young child would be adequate.

I am not going to give you an intense crash course here, but I will illustrate a few simple examples to whet your appetite. The first secret is that many words are the same or similar in English as Russian - how easy is that? The word "*Revolution*" for example is said in Russian "*Revolootsiya.*" (In Cyrillic it is революция) Did you notice the "в" is a "v"?

The second secret is the alphabet. It may look like gobbledygook now but what if I tell you a "я" says "ya", "л" is "l" and "д" is a "d." Confused? Don't be. Many of the letters are the same ones we know and love, let's look at A, M, K, O and T; they are the same letters in Cyrillic.

For example, when you are in Russia, at a café you will see the word "Кафе" – you already know that the "c" in the word café is the same as a hard "k" in English, the "К" is a hard "k" the same, and a "Ф" in Russian is an "f" in English, and the "a" and the "e" in *this* word are the same as ours. "Café" becomes "Кафе." You already learned some Russian!

The word "Russia" is almost the same, it is written "Россия." This is easily deconstructed also. The "Р" is a "R", the "о" is the same one you know, the "с" is an "s", so the double "сс" is as with English, and pro-

113

nounced "ss", the "и" is pronounced "ee" and the "я" is pronounced "ya." R-o-ss-ee-ya - Rosseeya is Russia!

Take a simple name like "Olga," in Russian Cyrillic it is "Ольга." The "O" is an "O" as you know it, the "л" is an "l" - the "г" is a "g" and the "a" is an "a" just the same! So "Ольга" is "Olga!" (The "ь" is not pronounced as such; it is a modifier symbol to indicate softening of the preceding consonant.)

Now you know that a Russian "C" is an English "S" and a Russian "P" is an English "R." So you now see that CCCP, (Russian for what we knew as the USSR - Union of Soviet Socialist Republics) is actually SSSR? It actually stands for *Soyuz Sovetskikh Sotsialisticheskikh Respublik*, (Сою́з Сове́тских Социалисти́ческих Респу́блик) but we won't delve any further into that in the confines of this book.

In this short lesson you learned Cyrillic A, M, K, O and T (the same as ours you cheat!), and you learned C (S), Я ("ya"), И ("ee"), Л (L), Ф (F), Г (G), and Р (R). I hope it now does not seem so daunting! Imagine what you could learn with a CD-Rom language course in only two hours.

If you want a Russian wife it is only respectful to try to learn some of her language. Maybe you will be terrible, but after this you will know a café when you see one! And maybe if it piques your interest you will be able to hold an amateur conversation in basic child-like language within a year. That is good enough. Nobody expects you to be word and tense perfect but at least you could order a beer for yourself and nobody would laugh at you, as you had a basic understandable grasp and was trying.

I can by now only string badly constructed sentences together, but I can be understood. I can have very elementary conversations with my

Overcoming Language Barriers

wife in Russian. She understands what I am trying to say. Native speakers sometimes chuckle at me with my Russian and I must resort to a translator or a dictionary, but I try. I am understood at a basic level and that most certainly does buy you some respect in Russia, and most especially with your woman.

It is valuable to have a basic grasp when you are listening to conversations. Much of what you hear will be gobbledygook, but when you can pick out a few words you can guess the structure of the sentence and its intent. If you heard what you understood as "yada yada plane, yada yada late, yada yada seven," you may well conclude, based on knowing only three words that the plane will be late and the person won't arrive until seven. You would probably be right and your Russian lady will be astonished.

Of course, in an ideal world everybody would speak English, but in reality they don't. If you take the trouble to learn some of her language, you will sympathize when she struggles with an aspect of yours and maybe be able to prompt her with the Russian word. English speakers are sometimes arrogant in their refusal to learn or even attempt other languages but for those that can make the effort, great rewards can be had, and more importantly, great women!

Consider also that after she has relocated to your country, her English will be developing for several years. During this time a rudimentary grasp of Russian will prove invaluable to you and your communication. Those of you with a thirst to learn more will find information on our resources website to assist you with this, including a link to a great free online series of lessons written by an American journalist we know who is married to a Russian woman and who spent several years living in Moscow.

Once again, decent communication with a zero or low English woman is a long hard road that will be quite frustrating for both of you at times. As obvious as it may sound, her language can only get better with time. The level of difficulty you experience at the beginning is as hard as it is going to get; the only way is onwards and upwards. Tell yourself that at the frustrating moments you will encounter when you are unable to explain something that is very important to you.

With an average women who has an English level of say 2/5 when you meet her, it will most likely take several months of frequent telephone calls, English tutoring and other language work to get her anywhere near a decent communication level and able to hold a half-decent conversation. It will take most women between one and two years of living in your country for her language to get to a standard that could be regarded as fluent. You must support your lady in every way possible as she learns your language. Do not forget she will be uprooting her life and leaving behind everything she knows to join you. Do not despair; she will keep her foxy foreign accent for many years to come!

Chapter Ten
Your First Meeting

Far too many men fall in love with a pretty face, long legs or an hourglass figure and jump straight on a plane, only to crash and burn when their illusions are rudely shattered. Perfection is illusory. The possibility that you may have found someone compatible enough and for whom you feel the initial chemistry and connection to create a good union must be investigated thoroughly by you. I cannot stress enough the need to get to know each other as much as possible via communication within a reasonably short timeframe before you meet.

Often when a man meets only one Russian woman, he will fall for her because she seems so much better than his local women. If you meet half a dozen Russian women you will have a much better perspective. It is generally recommended not to marry the first woman you meet. By meeting more than one Russian woman, you have a better chance of success.

It is very tempting to try to arrange your schedule to meet several women on one trip. How and if you tell the women you are doing this is your judgment call. Some women will accept this and appreciate your honesty; many will not and will dump you on the spot. I have always thought it must be difficult to explain to a lady when you are in her town, why you are sometimes unavailable. Trying to meet multiple women in the same town may backfire on you, especially if they share an agency. People talk, and your plan may come back to haunt you later on when you least expect it.

Many agency owners seem to be able to convince women to accept this "write many - visit many" approach. They impress upon them how much your flights cost and how they are orchestrating your initial meetings and generally sell them the idea. If you want to do this with women from the same agency, speak to the individual agency owner for advice in his town.

A more expensive method of achieving the same result is to visit women in multiple towns and cities on the same multi-stop visit. Four days in one town and four days in another seems to be a common way. The usual tale is that you are passing through on *business*. If she swallows your fairy tale or not is another matter altogether. If you meet more than one woman on a trip, you will probably have to lie to the women to do it without being dumped. You must again exercise your judgment as to whether lying in this manner is conducive to forming a lasting relationship.

The most effective and the more expensive route is to write to many women and visit one at a time. If one doesn't work out you just pick up with the next one in your list and go and meet her. This works better for self-employed people who can pick and choose their time off work. Explaining to the boss that you need another ten days vacation to fly to the FSU to go wife-hunting *again* is not a task many relish.

When you feel you have found *the one,* you obviously must get on an airplane and go meet her to determine if she may be right for you. If you decide she may be right for you, you will need to visit her a few more times before you consider marriage. If you have used up all your vacations, credible sick leave and favors to get to that point, further visits may be challenging. Many men must plan their visits with military style precision.

So now you have found a woman you want to visit. Now you are finally going to meet her in person for the first time. You will coordinate a suitable time for you and her, book your flights and arrange your accommodation. Now you need to prepare yourself physically and psychologically.

The first thing you must address is your personal grooming. It doesn't matter if you are an Adonis or an ugly duckling. You need to make the most of who you are and what you have. There are no shortcuts here. Do not underestimate the importance of the first impression you will make on your lady. Do not imagine that she won't notice every small detail about you.

A few days before you leave to meet her, you need to make the best of yourself. It will increase your self-confidence. Get a decent hair cut. Get rid of the nasal or ear hair you have. Cut your fingernails and toenails. If they are terrible, get a manicure or pedicure. If you have other dubious hair in unfortunate places get it waxed. Buy a quality pair of dress shoes. If your wardrobe is outdated, get a woman who is a friend, maybe the wife of a friend, to go with you to get some decent clothes.

Do not overlook anything. Pay attention to every area of your body and every item of your wardrobe. You are hoping to make the best possible first impression. Leave no stone unturned. If she is meeting you at your plane she will understand you may be a bit haggard from your flight, but you must still look your best. You should arrive as a picture of sartorial elegance and impeccable personal grooming.

Many Russian women are not too keen on beards and moustaches. It is something they often associate with old men. If there is a large age gap between you, it is like writing your differences on a banner for all to see when in Russia. If you are sporting facial hair, unless a cool five o'clock shadow on a well-chiseled face, I would suggest getting rid of it, or at least ask her honest opinion about it before you arrive. Young Russian women do not want to manhandle a handlebar moustache or grapple with Santa Claus' beard.

Some men dress badly; that is a fact. Russian women like men that dress well. Always dress to impress her. This is very important to many Russian women and in response Russian men are usually dressed very well. If you dress in old-fashioned or cheap clothes, the women will think that you are a cheap kind of man, and Russian women don't like cheap men. (Remember greedy?) They want men that can take care of them. If you cannot take care of yourself, they will think that you cannot take care of them.

If she is meeting you at the airport, make a plan as to how you will find each other. You don't want to be wandering about looking like a lost tourist looking for a woman who changed her hair color last week and you don't recognize from the old pictures you have. Make sure you have any and all contact numbers with you in case of difficulty.

When you meet, do not drool all over her. Kiss her hand or her cheek only or give her a gentle hug. Be subdued and do not over react physically. Be the perfect gentleman. Next you will probably get a taxi to your destination and check in your hotel or collect the keys to your apartment. After that, you will maybe go to a restaurant to get familiar and break the ice while all the shyness and foolish grinning wears off, and more importantly to see if you are able to communicate with each other adequately without assistance. Of course, if her English is limited, she may be accompanied by an interpreter when you first meet.

At some stage in your visit, the issue of sex will probably come up. Russian women generally are not too shy in that department, and if she likes you she will generally show you pretty quickly. It is worth noting that most of the FSU has quite high rates of AIDS, hepatitis and other unpleasant things you can catch all too easily, so use the same caution you would at home with regard to your personal safety.

Many Russian women are not too keen on the contraceptive pill due to potential weight gain and the high possibility of fake harmful pharmaceuticals that are rife in Russia. A traditional form of contraception in Russia - believe it or not - is abortion. It is not unusual for a woman in her twenties to have had several. If this subject ever arises, do *not* judge her by Western standards on this issue. If, during your visit, you feel the chemistry is there but sex does not happen, it is a fair bet (irrespective of the excuse), that this is a sign that she is not really interested in you.

Don't drink too much during your stay. Yes, beer and vodka is quite cheap in the FSU, but don't drink too much when you are with the woman you are dating. Russian women don't like the behavior of local men when they drink too much, so the last thing they want is a foreign man that drinks too much. If the woman refuses an alcoholic drink, then I recommend you don't drink yourself either. Bottled water is very cool and European.

Be a gentleman at all times. I cannot emphasize this point enough. I know that in Western Europe and the US we are not used to being gentlemen as much due to feminism and political correctness, but in the FSU men *are* gentlemen, and the women expect you to be one. Always help her with her coat; help her with the chair at restaurants, give her a helping hand out of cars; and open the door for her always. Always pay the bill at restaurants. If you ask her to split the bill at restaurants she will be very offended and you will be labeled "greedy" forever. Do not accept any partial contribution to the bill if offered. This is very important to FSU women. You must treat her like an old fashioned lady; the respect you will gain for this behavior will be incalculable.

I committed a major faux pas in the manners department when first in Russia. We were on a packed horrible little yellow *Marshrootka* bus, despite my protestations and expressed preference for a taxi. When it was time for us to exit, I was nearest the door in a bus crammed like a sardine tin and smelling badly of Yuri's armpits. Moving to one side to let my lady pass was out of the question, so when the moment came I exited first as seemed logical to me. Finding myself standing on the nearby pavement a few feet away alone prompted me to look around to see my lady holding the bus up, still standing at the exit with a very angry face. "Come on," I exclaimed, dumb as a brick. So she got off.

Then began my loud verbal lesson as to how a man should take his lady's hand as she exits the dreadful little bus. The fact that I neglected to do this seemingly inconsequential little thing created much sulking and ill-temperament for at least an hour. When I finally got to the bottom of it, it turned out she had seen a *Babushka* on the bus who knew her mother. She claimed my lack of gentlemanly demeanor would filter back to her mother. I laughed at the prospect, questioning if the Babushka would have even noticed, cared and would have been inclined to repeat such a trivial thing anyway.

The next day we were at her parents, a conversation broke out between my lady and her mother. I picked up only the words "bus," "Englishman" and my own name in this fast exchange. Yes, it turned out the Babushka had made a point of *bumping into* her mother and was most eager to recount the Englishman's lack of manners. Mother spent the afternoon giving me the *evil eye* and I spent the afternoon trying to be as gentlemanly as possible while her father was grinning and winking at me covertly. I didn't do that again.

Travel to the FSU is entirely different then traveling to the rest of Europe or America. The main language or second language is Russian of course, whereas in Western Europe, Australia, Canada and the States the usual first or second language is English. So traveling to the FSU will be much more difficult if you can't speak at least some Russian. Part of your planning, as mentioned, should be to learn as much Russian as you can before you go. It will make you trip much more interesting and you may be able to avoid some minor problems.

As I said earlier, abandon any idea she is coming to your country as a first meeting. She isn't! She probably can't get a visa; it would be too expensive for her if she could, and you are not going to pay in advance because you have already been cautioned about sending too much money to people you have never met. She can't afford to pay to travel to you, even if she had a visa, on the promise you will reimburse her when she arrives either. Just don't go there. Get it out of your head. You are going to her country.

In exceptional circumstances, you may be able to intercept her on a family holiday in Europe but at some stage, you *are* going there, probably many times, so get used to the idea. It is exciting. You are going behind what was once the Iron Curtain. You will be exposed to another culture and a new part of the world to you. This is fun and this is part of your future.

Some writings will have you believe that her hometown is the only place you should ever meet on the first occasion. This is not strictly true. In her hometown, she is subject to the scrutiny of her family, friends and work colleagues. As a foreigner, you will stand out like a sore thumb walking the streets with her and she may not want all the questions from people she knows about the foreign man they saw her walking with.

Often a woman will not tell her friends and family she is communicating with a foreign man or even that she has registered with an agency until she knows the relationship is going somewhere. Meeting in a third city or a mutually convenient location that may be near her hometown is acceptable for a first meeting. Her hometown is better for you as you want to see her in her natural habitat, but she may be more circumspect. If possible, visit her in her hometown; do not insist on it but aim toward it as an ideal. Be flexible on this issue and understand her motivation if she wants to meet you in Moscow or Kiev or some other larger city or town.

You must consider where you will stay on your visit. Will you stay with her? Probably not. What if you don't get along in person? You need a get-out-of-jail-free card and so does she. The best option is to ask her to

Your First Meeting

arrange a local apartment for you. You can stay in a hotel, but many FSU hotels want to charge you extra for overnight *guests* (assuming they are prostitutes and you will be happy to pay). If the object of your affection decides to spend the night with you, which we hope she will at some stage, it should be done without the scrutiny of nosy hotel staff which will make her feel uneasy and sometimes disinclined to spend the night with you, especially in her hometown. Russians are nosy; the local Babushka will be only too pleased to tell the neighborhood that Svetlana spent the night with a foreign man. She doesn't want that and neither do you. She has to live in that town after you have gone and she does not want to have to explain herself, nor have her reputation tarnished by gossip.

An apartment is better by far. Apartments are less expensive than hotels, especially if arranged by a local and you have total freedom of movement. Nobody clock-watching or sighing while opening doors late at night. Your lady will not be scrutinized by nosy staff or local Babushkas wondering about the local woman spending time with the foreigner. If you arrange an apartment on the internet, you may pay tourist prices. If she arranges your apartment, it will likely be significantly less and she will have the peace of mind knowing you will not be a burden to her if it does not work out. She will arrange it in a geographically convenient place for her home, work and family so you won't be marooned at the mercy of local taxi drivers grinning and emptying your pocket for each journey while taking the long route.

While you are there, don't be offended if she has to go to work. Two to four weeks vacation a year is average and she may have taken some already. Usually she won't be paid for her time off work. Remember, she needs that money to live. Do *not* make a big deal out of this if she has to work some days when you are there. Accept it; it is life there. If she has to work, you can walk around the town, visit the markets, practice your developing Russian language with locals and generally get familiar with the town and a feel for her country.

If she takes extra time off work to be with you, she will surely be losing money. She will be worried enough already about meeting you; adding financial burdens to that will not help. Find out or estimate what she earns and surreptitiously give her enough money to cover the lost salary somehow. It is not your intention to cause her financial hardship after you leave is it? "Oh, I exchanged too much money by mistake; you better take it, I can't use it" is a nice acceptable way to do this when you are leaving.

On my second meeting with my now wife, I visited her in her hometown. I was staying in her apartment. She had to work and she told me, "Don't go out, it's not safe for foreigners." Nevertheless, she left a key. Ten minutes after she left I was out on the streets, buying groceries, talking to people, getting involved, learning my way around the town, haggling with market sellers, etc.

She was very surprised when she came home; I had bought all the groceries we needed and knew the layout of the immediate area and was quizzing her on certain parts of it. I had met old men who spoke no English, but who were curious about the foreign man walking down their provincial street. I met Azerbaijani market traders. I spent some money with Babushkas selling flowers. I bought some bootleg MP3 albums not available elsewhere and I even had nice French wine in the fridge chilling when she got home. I was then her chameleon man, adaptable in all circumstances.

You must apply similar parameters to the first meet abroad as you would apply with any women. You know if all is going well; you know if the relationship will turn serious; you know if that closeness feels good and natural. This phase is no different than with any woman anywhere. The difference here is when you go home you must have made a plan to take it further; you also must have made a plan when you are going to see her next. She does not want to have met a sex tourist that says, "It's been nice; I will call you." She wants a plan and she wants to know when you will next come or when she will visit you. Do not leave without making a plan, assuming that you want to.

Do not make the mistake in May of saying to her, "I will see you in November." That is six whole months away; she doesn't want to wait six months until she next sees you. She is a serious girl, and she is looking for her second half, her husband. Assuming you have consummated your relationship, she wants a firm plan that does not involve six-month waits until she next sees you.

European men have the advantage here, they have only a four to nine hour travel time to anywhere in the FSU. Americans, Canadians and especially the poor Australians have a much harder task. They must travel ten plus hours and spend twice as much for a visit.

Your second meeting can be anywhere and might even be a small holiday. You must consider visa restrictions for her as to where she can travel. Egypt, Turkey, Israel and Cuba are good examples of easy places without onerous visa restrictions. (Americans currently have to fly elsewhere first to get to Cuba though.) This time you will be paying for her travel also.

She is now your lady; you are footing the bills. If possible, arrange e-tickets, tickets to be collected at the airport, or delivered by courier paid for at your end. Try not to get involved with her local travel agents; they quote one price but when she goes to pay, she will be hit for visa costs, commissions and other sundries that will be added. The cut-rate FSU travel deal will suddenly cost much more. I have tried and tested this method many times; each time our internet travel company was cheaper or at least within $50 of the final cost, and much safer. The only exception is internal flights on FSU airlines, they can often cost peanuts compared to what we would pay.

At this stage in your new relationship, it is acceptable to send her some money for the trip. If she needs an agent to arrange her visa for example, it may cost her $100 she does not have. This is your responsibility. Maybe she has to arrange a less costly local connecting flight to Moscow to connect to your second visit destination, she can arrange this locally at a good price. At this stage, don't sweat sending a reasonable amount of money if it is justified. Always add 20 percent for incidentals, as everyone in Russia adds all kinds of sundry charges at the last moment even she as a local may not be aware of. Even if not, you don't begrudge her a cup of coffee at the airport and some money in her pocket on her way through do you?

Your second meeting is great. You don't have the awkwardness like you had at the beginning of the first meeting; she knows now you are a serious-minded man and seriously making progress with a relationship with her. On the second meeting, you will both be much more relaxed

Your First Meeting

and more natural with each other. If her language was a problem before, she should have made some progress in that regard so it can only be better than the first time. During the second meeting, you will get to know each other much better and you will both be developing ideas about your suitability for each other over the long term. You will have the opportunity to enjoy each other's company.

As a side note - during your first and subsequent meetings, you must both keep as much proof as possible of your travels and meetings. Keep boarding passes, tickets, receipts from stores and restaurants, hotel paperwork, etc. You will need all these things and more later on to demonstrate you have a genuine relationship, in order to facilitate issue of her visa to your country.

If you are European, Canadian or Australian, by the end of your second meeting, you may be planning that she visits your country as the third meeting. She needs to see where she will live if you end up marrying; she needs to get a feel for your country and imagine herself living there.

Americans have a major disadvantage in this regard. A tourist visa to the US is very difficult to obtain and Americans must try to compensate for this during correspondence with more photographs of their locale and as much information on your area and way of life as possible. If you are American, probably the first time she will see your country is when she arrives on a fiancée or spousal visa. Until then, your country will be a complete unknown to her. This is a fact of life that Americans must work around.

Europeans and citizens of other countries have a better situation. If you can demonstrate that you have met already and are able to support her during her visit and she has overwhelming reasons to return to her country like children, family, employment, housing (preferably owned), etc., she will most likely receive a tourist visa to visit your country. There is more on the requirements in the visa chapter, but if possible, the next ideal stage is that she sees how you live and gets an impression of what her life will be like if she relocates and marries you.

Expensive as it may be, it cannot be over-emphasised that you should have as much face-to-face time as possible before making life-changing decisions such as marriage. The only way to do this is by visiting each other. It matters not for subsequent visits if you go to her, she comes to you or you meet in third countries. What matters is face-to-face time.

Never lose sight of the fact that you are choosing a life partner and are trying to compress the usual consideration period into days and weeks rather than months and years as you would with a local woman. Do not let a slim body, some good sex and your logistical constraints affect your judgment and cause you to propose marriage on the first visit. This is a grave error many people, especially Americans, make that often has far-reaching consequences. One man I know of after one visit proposed over Skype chat. This is clearly not recommended nor is it particularly romantic, although it may make an interesting after dinner anecdote in years to come.

Video calling or daily telephone calls are very nice and affordable, but this is not face-to-face time, nor should it be substituted for face-to-face time in your mind. While constant daily contact in a developing relationship is a must, nothing can or should substitute for face-to-face time. Now is where you both have to get creative to get time off work. She should be able to get a sick note from her doctor with no difficulty; many FSU doctors will overlook her obvious perfect health in exchange for a small contribution to their vodka fund and give her a sick note.

Remember, she will not be paid for time off work in this way; it will be up to you to reimburse her for her lost salary during these times. You may have to mask the payment as something else, or leave some money behind in "error" when you leave to achieve this. Handing her a wad of notes and saying, "Here is your lost salary, baby" is not recommended. She does not want to feel like a purchase and you will be quickly booted to the curb if you get this wrong.

After the first or second meeting is when it may be likely that you need to send her some money on a regular basis. This could be to get her international passport, pay for her internet connection or a myriad of other things that her salary will not stretch to that are now your responsibility anyway. Advance consideration should be given to this, in order that you are able to do it both efficiently and affordably.

Western Union is fine for the early couple of payments if you needed to pay for anything prior to your first meeting, but regular use will soon make you notice their charges, which can equate to as much as 14 percent.

Bank transfer is another option, but not all FSU women have bank accounts and their banks can sometimes levy charges on incoming international payments. Russian banks are notorious for rejecting payments if the slightest detail is wrong, even a spelling error in the detail. Simple bank-to-bank payments that you are used to are not always possible. Often you need the codes and details of one or two correspondent banks that the payment will route through. That can be troublesome.

The best way if she needs some money on a regular basis is a debit card from your country that works at her local ATM. Using a debit card or a similar specialized card will get you a decent exchange rate and a lower transaction fee than any other method.

The best method is to open a second basic checking account in your country that comes with a debit card that will work internationally. The fact it has your name on is not a factor as it will only be used in ATM cash machines. This way you can fund it as and when required. You will also be able to see the expenditure on your statements or on the internet. You must also notify your bank that the card is going to be used in the FSU, lest it may be rejected due to anti-fraud measures.

Your choice is limited to Visa and MasterCard if you want to supply her with a card that will be sure to work there. Discover, American Express, Maestro, Cirrus, Solo and others may only work with certain banks, if at all. Visa and MasterCard will work in most FSU banks.

A specialized pre-paid card is another option. There are several products that cater to this market and you will find links on our resources website for several.

Only supply a woman with a card if you are very certain that the relationship is going to prosper. Face-to-face time is critical to achieve that comfort level. A lot of face-to-face time is necessary, over several visits, before you make any serious decisions.

Nobody can tell you how much face-to-face time is enough with any particular woman. This differs for different people. It may take you two meetings or twenty. Do not make the commitment leap if you don't feel ready and don't make the mistake of thinking you can iron out any significant faults she has later on. If it doesn't feel right, it isn't right.

Trust your gut instincts and do not be afraid of pulling the plug if all is not going well. Yes, you may have to start all over again and spend thousands more finding and meeting another woman, but that is better than marrying an unsuitable woman and regretting it for many years to come. Beware of allowing your imagination to over romanticize your relationship when you are thousands of miles apart. Do not ignore negative character traits that may cause your relationship to unravel in the future.

Over the course of your quest, and certainly in the years to come, you will be visiting the FSU many times. The next chapter is about visiting the FSU.

Chapter Eleven
Visiting Russia

There is much written about Russia and the FSU that implies foreigners are not safe there. Overall, that simply is not the case. Some would have you believe that it is a land steeped in superstition, customs and behavioral expectations - not to mention the Mafia. You may hear that the errant foreigner who is not totally up to speed can expect to be marched up a dark alley by a man in sunglasses and a long dark coat, never to be seen again.

Russia and all FSU countries have their fair share of organized crime, but seldom will you ever come into contact with it unless you choose to open a business there or go out of your way to find it. The organized crime in Russia is mostly protection rackets and extortion from businesses at the lower levels. They often own the usual nightclubs and bars, similar to many other countries. The upper levels of organized crime are intermingled with big business and often involve politicians and other luminaries.

The Russian Mafia have absolutely no interest whatsoever in Joe Soap the tourist poking around looking to procure a local woman. As with any place, keep your money out of sight, do not dress too flashily and use common sense and you will never meet them. As long as you are frequenting reasonably safe towns, you can give the Mafia no further thought. The same goes for terrorists for that matter.

Of course, times change constantly in evolving territories and a place that is safe today may not be safe next year. Many war zones or hostile places later become tourist friendly. Kazakhstan is such a place. It was once firmly behind the iron curtain and shrouded in mystery, but is now a tourist hot spot thanks to the comedy character Borat of all people. However, at the time of writing, Chechnya and Turkmenistan are places, which probably should be avoided. Usually, the accepted technique with a woman from such a place is to meet in a third safer location and continue to do so. In that situation, you may disregard the meeting in her hometown I drilled into you earlier as an ideal.

Pay attention to the world media; avoid areas of obvious conflict or third world abject poverty and anywhere that foreigners are deemed unsafe. Often your country's government will have a website with government recommendations for travelers to everywhere. Treat this information as advisory though; it is subject to bureaucratic manipulation and this week's political motivation, and cannot always be relied upon as gospel. If in doubt, it is better to locate an online forum or community of people who actually travel there. They will know better.

For the most part, readers of this book will be searching in mainland Russia and its enclaves and reasonably tourist friendly places like Ukraine and the Baltic States. In these places, any seasoned traveler with his wits about him will be fine.

You should be aware of etiquette and superstitions in the country you plan to visit. Russians are quite superstitious, especially the women. They may pay all kinds of attention to astrology, the moon cycles and a whole host of other things. You will read elsewhere about how you must strictly observe superstitions relating to one's social behavior. You should have a working knowledge of Russian superstitions and respect them even if you find them humorous. If you neglect some nobody will care too much in this day and age. Your actions will probably be written off as an ignorant foreigner, but observance of some will serve to demonstrate that you took the trouble to find out about her culture a little, and will please her. A few of the more common superstitions you will encounter are below:

- Men in Russia will always shake hands when they greet for the first time during that day. However, it is taboo to shake hands with your gloves on. A glove must be removed, no matter how cold it may be. This is more regarded as good etiquette rather than superstition.

- Sitting on cold surfaces, such as rocks or even the ground, is not merely taboo for a woman, but is believed to be quite hazardous to health and is believed to inhibit her ability to have children. It is a practice that is rigorously upheld, especially in cold weather and with young children, who will often unknowingly sit on the ground, and who will frequently be lifted up by a scowling parent.

- Shaking hands and giving things across a threshold is taboo. Usually a guest will come inside before shaking the host's hand when arriving, and shake it before leaving the threshold when leaving. Sometimes people will even avoid saying "hello" and "goodbye" across a threshold.

- It is traditional in Russia for men to give flowers to women on every special occasion, and there are many occasions, some not so special. But only an odd number should be given. Giving an even number of flowers is only for funerals. This is a big one, remember it!

- When you are invited to someone's home, you should always take a gift. You should never go to someone else's house empty-handed. Alcoholic beverages, flowers, chocolate or some other small gift for the house demonstrate good manners. The cost is unimportant; it's the thought that counts.

- It is impolite to point with your finger. But if you must point, it's better to use your entire hand instead of your finger.

- Etiquette dictates that shoes are removed when entering someone's home. Often the host will have several pairs of guest slippers.

- Whistling indoors is not advised. Russians say that you will "whistle away your money."

- Traditional Russian cheek kissing is done using three kisses, but this is not upheld all the time; often you will encounter a European two cheek kiss.

- When someone sneezes you tell them "bud'te zdorovy" (Будьте здоровы), which literally means "be healthy." It used to be believed that saying this would prevent the sneezer from getting sick. Russian speakers will say it freely just as an English speaker may say "bless you."

- Before leaving for a long journey the traveler, and all those who are seeing him off, must sit for a moment in silence before leaving the house. It is often conveniently written off as a time to sit and think of anything one may have forgotten, but is said to bring luck on the journey.

- After someone has left the house on a long journey, their room and their things should not be cleaned up until they have arrived at their destination, or sometimes not for three days after.

- Birthday parties should be celebrated on or after one's birthday, not before. So when one's birthday falls during the week, it's best to celebrate the following weekend.

- Returning home for forgotten things is a bad omen. It is better to leave it behind if you can, but if a return visit is necessary, one should look in the mirror before leaving the house again. Otherwise, it is believed, the journey will be bad.

- Things bought for a newborn baby should only be purchased after the baby is born.

- Unmarried people shouldn't sit at the corner of the table, otherwise they won't marry. This mostly applies to girls, and often only young girls. Sometimes it is said that you will not marry for seven years, making it acceptable for young children to sit there.

- A purse or wallet given as a gift should have a little money inside. Given empty, it is said to cause financial bad luck.

- A stranger should not look at a newborn baby before it is a certain age, usually two months old. If you see a pram in the street with the open part obscured by lace, now you know why this is.

The list above is far from exhaustive, but gives you a general idea. I have met non-superstitious Russians who laugh at *most* of the above and ones who seem to live their life with these and more superstitions becoming almost a burden. The main superstitions that seem to be non-negotiable are the odd number of flowers, women sitting on cold surfaces, threshold greetings and sitting before a journey. Your experiences may differ however. In my research I found some my wife had never heard of. When asked about them she replied, "Nobody does this any more; it's just an old wives tale," as if to shrug off all superstition. I then found her sitting for two minutes before she went out! Many of these superstitions tend to be slowly forgotten by women who have relocated abroad, so don't worry that you will have to live your life with this seemingly illogical behavior forever.

You maybe should mark in your diary March 8th. That is International Women's Day. This is much more important than Valentine's Day in Russia. It is a day to celebrate women and all they represent in society. On this day your lady (or potential lady and probably her mother too) should have a gift from you; flowers are the most traditional gift. Forget or overlook this day and most women will treat it as a major sign of disrespect. There is a link on our resources website to other events in the Russian calendar you may need to know about, but International Women's Day is by far the most important one for you to remember.

So superstitions, events and basic social etiquette aside, what else should you be aware of when visiting Russia?

EU, US, Canadian citizens and folks from Australia no longer need a visa to travel to the Baltic States or Ukraine. Currently, everyone needs one for Russia and some of the CIS countries. Although upon first investigation it sounds difficult to get, in reality it is a breeze. To get a Russian visa I recommend one of the many visa agents that are around; there are several listed on our resources website. Their fees are minimal and they arrange your support paperwork meaning you have less to worry about.

Your support paperwork for Russia and some other CIS countries basically consists of two documents, a tourist voucher and a hotel reservation confirmation. Technically, they show you have reserved and paid for a hotel and are invited by an official body of some kind, usually a travel agent. These papers are a carryover from Soviet days. Nobody will check or care if you stay in the hotel detailed; if asked, you just say you are.

If you use a visa agent, they will supply these bits of paper so you don't need to consider them. If you choose to apply directly to the embassy yourself, Google will yield many places authorized to issue them by e-mail for maybe $60. The support paperwork thing is basically a pointless racket allowing bureaucrats to justify their existence shuffling bits of paper around and rubber stamping things, and for a few people to make a little money.

When entering most FSU countries, you need to fill out a landing card. You get them either on the plane before you land or at the airport itself. If they are in Cyrillic only, your airline will have a translation form to guide you or just ask a flight attendant. The form is all basic: Personal information, purpose of the visit, where you will be staying, etc. For Russia, it is obligatory to fill in the name and the address of the inviting com-

Visiting Russia

pany, all of which should be provided in your visa support paperwork.

After arrival in Russia you must have your migration card stamped within three working days (visa registration) lest you be considered an illegal. This gets done either by your hotel, or at a Post Office with your lady's assistance. The local travel agent can sometimes oblige or sometimes your visa agent will arrange it. Ask your visa agent if unsure as Russia tweaks these rules occasionally and its best to be up to date.

You can also go to the OVIR (Office of Visas and Registration) with your lady if you are staying with her, or in some towns you must go to the Passport and Visa Department of the local police precinct. The Post Office, travel agent or hotel option seem to be the favorite of regular travelers.

Foreign visitors may also be asked upon entry how long they intend to spend in Russia and may be asked to show proof such as return tickets. However, most foreigners are admitted without any problems at all, as long their answers to any questions correspond with the information on the visa and visa support documents.

As with many things in Russia, the border control can be slow and the entry process is subject to much fervid rubber stamping of things, executed to make it all seem very important. When you enter, you will be given some piece of paper, often a part of your landing card, which you must keep with your passport. Do not lose this piece of paper. It will be handed over to immigration officials when leaving the country.

When you arrive in a Russian or Ukrainian airport and clear passport control and customs, you walk out into the public area toting your baggage. At this point, you will be positively besieged by taxi drivers. The taxi drivers are most famously aggressive in Moscow Sheremetyevo airport, but you will find rancid smelling Ivan's surreptitiously puffing on a cigarette waiting to ambush foreigners and bundle them into an overpriced dirty Lada at most FSU airports. These guys don't like to take no for an answer, so look stern and say, "Nyet," while pushing past them.

Many of you will be connecting through Moscow Sheremetyevo; it has two terminals SVO1 and SVO2. International flights arrive in SVO2 and domestic flights depart from SVO1. The two terminals are about three miles apart; which explains the taxi driver scramble to relieve the unsuspecting foreigner of $50 or more to travel between them.

If you are flying with Aeroflot or a member of Sky Team Alliance, they have a transit desk in the arrivals hall and provide a free transit bus. You do have to ask. Find the kiosk for Aeroflot; show the woman your ticket for your domestic Aeroflot flight. She will then give you an orange transfer ticket. Go outside to the second set of traffic islands. You will see a yellow sign that says SVO1 - SVO2. Wait there and the bus will take you to SVO1 for free.

If you are flying with another airline, fight your way through the taxi drivers, then outside you need to find the big bus with number 817 to transfer from SVO2 to SVO1, and 851(c) from SVO1 to SVO2. The cost of the bus is around $2 and any of the above buses takes twenty minutes to get from one terminal to the other. Have Russian Rubles already (about fifty) as the drivers won't accept foreign money, dislike giving change from big Russian notes and seldom speak English.

There are two other Airports around Moscow, Vnukovo (VKO) located eighteen miles southwest from the center of Moscow, and Domodedovo (DME) located twenty-two miles south of the centre of Moscow. If you need to transfer between different Moscow airports, try to arrange a driver in advance who will be waiting for you with a sign and who will charge you a previously agreed fixed price. The internet will yield many such services. There are express trains from Paveletskaya station to DME airport and from Kievskaya station to VKO airport also.

It is always preferable to have your lady meet you at your ultimate destination airport if logistically possible; she can smooth the way for you. In the absence of her, your previously arranged driver, agency representative or other suitable person will assist you to a money change kiosk and onward to your destination.

Do not use random taxi drivers anywhere at first until you know the ropes and can speak some Russian. In Russia, anyone with a car can be a taxi, no registration required. Just stand by the side of the road with your arm out and somebody will stop. Agreeing the price to your destination before you get in is the norm, lest you be taken on a magical mystery tour and have to argue with a big Ivan at the end of the journey. Having agreed a price, try to have the correct money, as he will claim he has no change. Tipping is not required or expected.

Your first journey on the roads will surprise you a little. Russians drive in a terrifyingly self-destructive manner. All cars are the same color most of the year, sprayed with a cement colored coating of mud and road film. You will smell the exhaust gases from everything around you and it will stick in your throat. This will pass in a few days and the feebler amongst you will have a sore throat from the pollution in many places for a day or two. I do not recommend driving in Russia for the uninitiated, certainly not for the first time visitor, so forget about rental cars.

Russia is predominantly still a cash-based society, so abandon thoughts of using your credit cards everywhere. You need cash in Russia. Big name international cards should work in most cash machines (ATMs) but don't count on it. It is better to have ample cash to cover your needs and any eventualities. Many shops that advertise they accept cards will suffer from a "broken machine" if you try to use your card. Either they never took them at all and just wanted to look good with a window full of signs or they will try to refuse them in favor of cash.

Cash is mostly untaxed, and Russians don't like paying taxes. So pay cash if you want to be sure. Cash means local currency only; seldom will you find stores willing to take Euros, Sterling or US Dollars. Dollars have lost favor somewhat due to volatility of that currency in recent years. Most FSU currencies are relatively stable nowadays, so dependence on other currencies is less important. If you find a foreign currency used anywhere in the FSU it will most likely be Euros. Money change outlets will accept any major currency. An important point about money is that the foreign currency that you exchange needs to be in good condition. Money that is dirty or dog-eared or with writing on it will be segregated and you will be offered a lesser exchange rate on it if it is accepted at all. Try to amass nice clean, preferably new notes of your currency before you go.

When eating out, or in fact in most places, tipping is not necessary. I shall repeat that again for Americans; tipping is not necessary. If you tip, you will be instantly regarded as a foreigner with money to give away. However, if you want to do so, do it based on service levels only. Russians have been trying to encourage a tipping culture in recent years but they mostly haven't correlated in their heads the concept of service to the size of tip.

Russian service generally is way short of the European mark and dismally short of the US mark. In the tourist spots you will often find a service charge of 10 percent is sometimes added to your bill, so in this instance you're not expected to tip more anyway. If you really want to tip, 5-10 percent is more than enough, and if you feel that strongly about it, try to tip the server personally.

Russia is still extremely corrupt, slow and bureaucratic. Most things you want to do will involve a long wait and a plethora of rubber stamps on innumerable pieces of paper administered by people who have been to the school of how to look stern and serious. Any small thing that could be performed by one person in minutes invariably involves six people, two hours (or weeks and months for some things) and multifarious paperwork.

That can be anything from changing money in a bank, getting your heating repaired or posting a letter. Expect things to be slow and take time. The best way to jump some waiting lists is to pay the person who administers it; your lady will be an expert at this since it is part of life all over the FSU. Do you want your passport today and not next month? Do you want the cops to overlook your traffic violation? Do you want your heating repaired before next summer? Money is the simple answer to all these small problems and most others. Money talks in Russia; the more money it is, the louder it talks.

Some say Russians are miserable because everyone on the streets and in the shops look so serious and nobody is smiling; this is not so. You don't find the "have a nice day" stuff that is normal in the States and you don't find staff falsely grinning in shops. The fact is Russians do not smile for no reason; they smile when they have something to smile about.

Inane grinning in shops and on the street is considered foolish and a habit of foreigners. Relocated Russians usually come to enjoy the smiling that we associate with good service and polite behavior, but Russians still in Russia will seldom do it. Catch a girl's eye in the street and the best you will get is a smoldering look and maybe a hint of a smirk; if she grins at you then she is probably a tourist too.

When you are out and about in Russia you should always carry your passport (or a clean photocopy of the identification page) with you at all times. There is always a small possibility that you will be stopped by the police (known as the militia) and they will ask for your documents. When they say "document" they basically mean any decent photographic identification, usually your passport.

The police in Russia and indeed most of the FSU, even the EU parts, are not the pillars of society they are in much of the West. Corruption is endemic and to be expected. This is mostly from the traffic police who you will not encounter if you don't drive, but street militias are prone to check peoples' documents. Naturally they sometimes like to find a reason why they should be bribed to allow you to continue unhindered.

How you handle this depends on your personality and where you are. If you are in a small dark street at night and there are three of them, the line of least resistance is advised; pay them a modest bribe and continue your evening unmolested. If in the middle of the day on a busy street in a big town or city, make some noise about calling your embassy or consulate. Or maybe start writing their numbers down and asking for their identification; they will probably just give you back your passport and allow you to continue and seek an easier mark. Not all will be corrupt in this way but enough of them are to make it noteworthy.

One should avoid being drunk in the street; staggering along alone, inebriated and encountering a militia patrol is liable to get you beat up and your pockets emptied and your valuables stolen. Quite often in the evening the militias are drunk themselves and thus prone to such "errors of judgment." Drunken gun-toting militias are best avoided. If you are lost and need directions, ask a sexy young lady, not a militia. If confronted by them, be polite yet firm. Do not always assume the worst. If you must bribe them do not pay the asking price but negotiate. Do not accept offers to accompany them to the police station in their car unless you have actually done something wrong you can identify. In most cases, if you can prove your identity and are doing nothing wrong there is no reason for concern.

So what does Russia actually look like? Well, it doesn't snow all the time. Nobody wears fur hats with a red star on the front (except tourists), and there are no bears in the streets or bread queues as the media still sometimes portrays. When I first went, the first word that came into my mind was "grey." Streets, buildings, cars and old men's faces all seem to look grey. It can be like watching an old black and white movie.

The well-dressed glamorous ladies provide a most welcome splash of color and against this backdrop they become even more noticeable. The streets will be awash in most places with many good-looking, sexilydressed ladies who all look as if they are on their way to a fashion shoot. You have to admire a nation of women who can wear stilettos in the snow and make it look simple. It can be minus fifteen degrees, and the frozen pavements in some cities can be wall to wall with glamorous females. They can expertly navigate the ice in four-inch heels; you must see it to believe it. Try not to stare, you will get used to the phenomenon of abundant attractive women in all weathers. An English friend of ours who lives in the FSU calls this particular year-round visual feast "moving wallpaper."

It is more than likely that the women you will be meeting will be regular working or middle-class girls. As such she will most likely live in an apartment, sometimes still with her parents. Many families had an apartment given to the them or a relative under Soviet rule. They are typically quiet small, usually between one and three rooms total plus a small kitchen and bathroom. Sometimes the living room will double up as a bedroom with the use of a sofa bed.

Heating is usually communal in the building and the radiators are often big cast iron affairs like you see in Victorian schools or factories. Hot water gushing through wide pipes into cast iron radiators in small apartments makes for very hot apartments. When you consider that instead of a thermostat, a big "on" and "off" tap is more common, this explains why most Russian apartments are heated excessively.

The older grey concrete apartment buildings you will see everywhere were constructed in Soviet times. Construction quality is poor by Western standards; a large steel door that opens outwards with a five-inch key lets you to the concrete stairs with metal handrails, usually with chipped half and half two-color paintwork. Some high-rise apartments have creaking old elevators; many don't. Some buildings have a little office situated just inside the main door where a collection of old women (Babushkas) sit all day as caretakers watching who comes and goes. Unknown people may be questioned about why they are there.

The affluence of the inhabitants will dictate how much the apartment has been upgraded since Soviet days. Many apartments have outward opening steel doors with many locks. Yet, inside, many apartments have well-designed kitchens with modern appliances, laminate floors, double-glazed windows and most creature comforts. The more impecunious Russian will live in more basic conditions. Space or the lack thereof, is what most Westerners will notice about older Russian apartments. I have seldom been in a dirty apartment though; irrespective of décor, it will most likely be very clean and well-organized.

As Russia's prosperity increases, more and more new apartments are being built. The new apartments are comparable with any European apartment in size and specification. Mortgages and home loans are still in their infancy and at high interest rates in Russia. Most people either rent or own their apartment outright. It can be difficult for a young family in Russia to get on the property ladder due to the inflation in recent years.

Many families have a dacha or a summer house. This is usually a small wooden country home on a small piece of land where Russians spend much time in the summer, close to nature, growing vegetables, swimming, having barbeques, etc. The dacha is a place to relax and unwind and get out of the city. Often people have a small barter system going on in the small weekend dacha communities (rather like English allotments) where, for example, a man who has grown many apples will swap some with one of the neighbors for some honey, gherkins or something else. Many things are grown at dachas and stockpiled for the coming months. Quality is often superb and we always bring some Russian honey back to England from our family dacha by the Volga River. If you are invited to the dacha by a woman and her family, you are well regarded and almost one of the family.

Not everyone has a car in Russia; most use public transportation. That would either be the Metro (underground train or subway if her city has one), bus or taxi. Those that do have a car increasingly prefer European and especially Japanese cars. The patriots that the Russians are though, the Russian made cars Lada and Volga still have mass appeal. Laugh at them if you want (not in front of your woman though), but they do still work at -25c.

If you take the bus it will often be a small van-based mini-bus called a "Marshrootka" or one of the bigger old creaking 1960s buses and trolleys you will see that can look like a patchwork quilt of colors, often with the engine flap propped open with a piece of wood. Big buses are not pretty, but they are cheap.

Most people you encounter will be quite friendly. Russians are good hosts and will empty their cupboards of food to offer a visitor a lavish spread. For some reason, Russians have a reputation of being unfriendly. I don't know why. Maybe it is some left over cold-war propaganda still remaining in our heads.

The only unfriendly Russians you will encounter are usually those behind glass windows or more generally those who have to sell you something. They can be deliberately unhelpful. This can be disturbing for a Westerner who is used to getting a complimentary smile with every item purchased. As with any country in the world, there are friendly people and there are miserable ones.

Russia has a reputation for being a poor second-world country; this is something else that is rapidly changing. Russia is a land of contrast where you will see old women who look homeless begging for money alongside a man who has just pulled up in the latest S-Class Mercedes he paid cash for.

As Russia's economy grows, the gap between rich and poor is larger and thus more visible. Many modern Russians are quite affluent as Russia embraces its own unique brand of democracy, although the state does not look after its poor and its pensioners with social programs as is common in the West. If a Russian has money, he will love to flaunt it.

A popular anecdote about two "new Russians," both of whom have recently bought a tie, is a case in point. "Mine cost 500 rubles," says one man. "That's nothing," says the other man looking at his tie which looks rather similar to his friend's. "Mine is much better; it cost 2,500 rubles."

The tie story is something indicative of some attitudes you will encounter in women. Many believe unless an item costs a lot of money it must be of poor quality. The concept that somebody is probably just overcharging you is only just dawning on Russians. This is an attitude you will have to tread carefully around lest you be labeled "greedy" as mentioned elsewhere. It will take a woman a while to appreciate the concept of value-for-money with consumer goods.

Visiting Russia or any former Soviet Union country is a unique experience you will never forget. It is not something to be looked at with trepidation or something you should try to avoid. Enjoy Russia for what it is; don't criticize it because it may not be what you think it should be. See its good points and appreciate its history, culture and most especially its gorgeous ladies.

Chapter Twelve
Maintaining Long-Distance Relationships

Maintaining and strengthening your relationship with a Russian woman while you are far away in your homeland will require a serious effort on your part.

This is another good reason why SMS and telephone contact should be established and maintained on a *daily* basis. You are trying to create and maintain a spark over thousands of miles; you must make sure that you are in her mind each day for a fair portion of the day.

Telephone, e-mail, SMS (text message), mail her postcards and letters, pop up on her internet messenger, have a small gift, maybe some flowers, delivered. It is your responsibility to become a necessary and desirable part of her daily life. Plus, if she is sitting in a café with Ivan, it is quite difficult to explain the incoming English language call from abroad or a flurry of SMS messages on a Saturday evening. Maybe Ivan will be too much effort for her to maintain as you are so attentive and beginning to arrive in person quite frequently anyway.

Only after your actual arrival, and assuming you hit it off, can you consider her to be your girlfriend; only then can you take a more detailed interest in her movements. Before this, she is only your pen pal. Do not expect she will take any less interest in your social activity either. When you are "her man" in her mind, is when you can expect an impromptu short call from her at your home on a Saturday evening.

Woe betide you if you don't answer the phone after telling her you were home with a microwave meal for one watching sports on TV all evening. Worse still for you would be if your local female temporary companion answers the telephone passing en route to the kitchen for a corkscrew! Thousands of miles apart you may be, but neither of you are stupid. Remember, Russian men are well known serial philanderers; she will already know every trick in the book to insure your fidelity. A few thousand miles will make little difference to that.

Your home country and respective personal circumstances will determine how long between visits you both have to wait to see each other. The time between visits is often the killer factor. After all your mutual efforts to build a relationship, this is the period you should be giving extra special consideration to. Many relationships fail during this period.

Sometimes a man with bad planning runs out of money and vacation time and is unable to commit to his next visit. If she does not feel you are in her life every day and a real part of her life, there is the possibility that the affections of a local Ivan or another foreign man may take precedence over yours. Now is the time you must be the man with a plan.

The point in time when you have decided she is the one for you is when you will more than likely be popping the question and asking her to marry you. Assuming it gets an initial "yes" from her, the concept usually still has to pass through the committee that is her family. This will have probably been done well in advance with a foreign man anyway and she will know their feelings already.

In the old days, a man was expected to visit the parents and ask for their permission for their daughters hand in marriage; refusal would mean going home with only a pumpkin to show for his efforts. Even today,

Maintaining Long-Distance Relationships

parents can veto the marriage if they really want to. This is highly unlikely if you are all on good terms, especially since they consider you to be a wealthy Westerner who has plenty of resources to care for their daughter.

By now you should be getting fully conversant with the rules and regulations and more importantly processing times of visa applications to your country. If you are not European, you may well have to wait up to a year for the issue of her fiancée visa as you will find out in the next chapter.

During this time you both should be communicating daily and making absolutely sure that you are heading in the direction you both want. You should be also seeing each other face-to-face a few more times if at all possible before the big relocation.

If a woman was listed with an international introduction agency that matches women with foreign men then it logically suggests that, unless she is dumb as a brick, that she has made certain choices already and is willing to make certain compromises with herself. One of those choices or compromises is that the man she is seeking is likely to be from another country. So in furtherance to that she has already decided she will live abroad. That makes sense doesn't it?

It may make perfect sense to us but not always to Russian women. Leaving Russia is often a huge sacrifice for them. At this stage some of them will try to convince you to live in Russia or their FSU country. For them it seems perfectly reasonable that you would consider it. I know one or two men who have actually done this, or lived between two countries.

On the whole it doesn't work, mainly because the source of your income that made this all happen is derived from whatever you do in your country. Few men are of independent means or with a suitably portable trade or occupation to be able to do this, even if they wanted to. So you must gently let her down on this front and explain all the reasons why it cannot be, and get her used to the idea that she will be moving to your country.

Howling with laughter and proclaiming, "Why the hell would I live in this god-forsaken place?" is not the way forward here; diplomacy is. Remember, for all its faults, she loves her country very much. Most Russians are fiercely patriotic; the fact that so many live abroad has nothing to do with this and does not alter this view. Our perspective of Russia differs greatly from theirs; disrespect her Motherland at your peril.

Discuss with her all aspects of her forthcoming relocation. Make sure she is psychologically prepared for it. Make sure you have the approval of her parents as their support will give her great strength for what she has to come. Never lose sight of the fact that by moving abroad, marrying and creating a new family with you, she will also be leaving behind the only family she has ever known. This is a tremendous personal issue for most women and the psychological effect on her now and after relocation cannot be underestimated.

In addition to her family, she will also be leaving behind the streets she grew up in, her friends, her work and everything that is familiar and secure to her. She is going to a country where she will seldom speak in her native tongue. She has to learn new customs, routines and so many things that she may feel inadequate and frustrated in her new country for a while. It takes enormous strength of character and a lot of trust in you to enable her to do this.

Maintaining Long-Distance Relationships

When women first join an agency, they often do not think of the time they will actually be planning to leave Russia. Often they join for a laugh, just to see what the possibilities are. Sometimes it can be just to get some attention or because their friend is doing it so they think to themselves, "Why not?" It is rumored, and perpetuated by the Russian media, that only fat old Americans seek Russian wives, so women are often totally unprepared if they meet and develop feelings for a nice compatible man. Suddenly one day after accepting his proposal, he wants to talk about her relocation and the alarm bells sound in her head.

If she has had the opportunity to visit your country on a tourist visa, you can breathe a little easier. She has already seen your house, your life, your country and had chance to sit and think about it and consider her future. If she hasn't, she is agreeing to moving continents effectively blindfolded, and that takes a tremendous leap of faith to do.

If she has a child then she has to consider the future of the child also. This will usually tip the scales as most women will recognize that their child will have more opportunity and a completely different life abroad than they will in Russia.

If she has a child, you must from the beginning have been demonstrating what a wonderful father figure you are, and not have been shy lavishing attention on her child also. It will be difficult for her to accept that a man, even a foreign man, will accept someone else's child as his own. This seldom happens in Russia, so she may take some convincing. In this case, your actions over time speak louder than words ever could.

After she has agreed and is happy that she is coming to your country, it is the time to take some practical steps. She may well have heaps of stuff in Russia like books, clothes and all kinds of things she will want to bring with her. As most international flights only allow 20-25 kilos before punitive excess baggage charges kick in, it can be advantageous on your visits to bring a little back with you each time.

If you can find a good deal with a courier from her country to yours on the internet, you might suggest she start shipping books and low value things incrementally this way. It will be cheaper than excess baggage penalties when she does come. I have heard about many men who received an emergency phone call from their woman at her departure airport crying because the airline wanted to charge her hundreds for excess baggage.

Getting a few of her bits and pieces to your place in advance is an important step I feel. When some of her things are in your house it will start the psychological moving process for you both. A small part of her has arrived in your life already. A useful side factor is that in your daily telephone conversations it gives you other things to discuss that can only assist in expanding her English vocabulary. You must be able to discuss everyday mundane things with her, lest she will find it very difficult to communicate when she arrives on topics that expand beyond love, sex and fluffy subjects.

This period of communication during the long distance relationship phase is when you should seize the opportunity to expand her language as fast as possible. This is when you should be funding intensive English lessons and a fast internet connection. Get her onto VOIP and webcam calling if you haven't done so already; not only will it be free, thus drastically reducing your long distance phone bills, but when she leaves, she can teach her parents how to use this technology then she can speak with them and even see them daily. Seeing each other every day over a webcam, while no substitute for actual face-to-face contact, is often the next best thing.

By the time she is ready to relocate, her English should have improved substantially due to your joint efforts and all should be rosy in the garden. She has accepted and prepared for her new life with you; she has the support of her family. It is time to plan for her arrival and plan for her visa, if you haven't done so already.

Chapter Thirteen
Visas

When you have decided that you have met the one you will marry and she feels the same about you, then it is time to wade through the morass of paperwork that your government, regardless of your country, will require.

As with many things controlled by governments, the rules governing visas change often, so I will give you a brief overview of the principles, and a brief summary for several countries as of the time of writing. You must do your own research into the situation in your country.

There are two general ways to get your chosen lady legally into your country. The first option is for her to obtain a fiancée visa which allows her a fixed time in your country, usually three to six months, sometimes nine depending on country. At the end of this time she must be married to you in order to apply for semi-permanent residence status (on the basis of being married to a national). The application for post-marriage residence can usually be made from within your country in this case.

The alternative route is for you to marry abroad, usually in her country. Where you actually marry does not really matter, so long as it is an internationally recognized wedding. Then, from her home country, she must apply to the embassy of your country for a visa to join her husband in his homeland. (This is the only option for Canadians; they do not issue fiancée visas.)

The fiancée visa is a residence permit of sorts; when you marry, she gets a further residency period. If she stays married, then at some future point, she will be able to get permanent residency and later apply for a passport from your country.

If you marry abroad, her residency is usually not technically an automatic right. You still must jump through some hoops to demonstrate to the authorities that your relationship is genuine and not just an immigration scam.

There are subtle differences in the rules as to what one must do to qualify for a fiancée visa versus a post-marital residence visa for a person married abroad. In Europe, there is much less financial scrutiny generally for a post-marital residence visa than a fiancée visa.

If she has children, visas must be obtained for them also. There is nothing overwhelming about this process except the predictable extra costs and the fact that the birth father of the children must give his permission for them to emigrate. If the father cannot be found, then usually a judge must grant permission. This is quite routine. A bribe may be necessary to oil the wheels of *justice*.

If the father is around and involved in their lives, he may kick up a fuss and could conceivably block it altogether. Here you have two options; he must be bribed to agree and sign the documents, or tied up in court proceedings he likely cannot afford to contest.

There are many creative ways around this which should have been discussed with your woman well before the application stage. You don't want father blocking little Ivan's relocation, which would usually put the brakes on your fiancée's relocation by default. Address this issue early on with her, when you first get serious. If the moral question of removing a child from his natural father troubles you, find a childless woman or be totally sure about the situation before you get too far down the road with her.

There are no shortcuts in the visa procedure. Each country will have its own rules and regulations and its own requirements. It will be up to you to conform to your country's procedures. Individual embassy websites are usually quite informative; some countries even have the information in Russian. You will find links to many on our resources website. Below are the general guidelines and procedures for a few popular countries.

THE UNITED KINGDOM OF GREAT BRITAIN & NORTHERN IRELAND

All applications are handled by UK Visa Application Centers, (VAC) of which there are three in Russia; Moscow, St Petersburg and Ekaterinburg. If your lady is from a country other than Russia itself, you will have to determine where her local VAC is.

Applications are to be made exclusively on-line. Having completed the on-line application form, you will be prompted to book an appointment to submit your application. It is necessary for the applicant to visit the Application Centre in person. A relative, friend or representative cannot submit the application. All UK visa applicants are required to provide both finger scans and a digital photo as part of the application process. These finger scans and digital photos are your biometric data.

You must be able to prove that your lady qualifies for a visa and that you can support her in the UK without her initially working or claiming public money. In short, if you have somewhere to live, have a decent job or have some savings (or even demonstrable credit facilities), and can prove that you've met your lady more than once, it's a breeze.

If a fiancée or settlement visa, the applicant and her sponsor (you) need to provide documentary evidence of an ongoing and genuine relationship. This should include things like copies of correspondence between you, photographs of the two of you together, flight and train tickets, accommodation receipts, evidence of wedding plans, e.g., letter from your vicar, Registry Office, or the venue where you are holding your wedding reception. Any documents received in Russian must be translated, notarized and include the original copy in Russian also.

The UK is not too difficult, provided that the sponsor and applicant provide all the required documents, the sponsor is able to show that he is financially solvent and present and settled in the UK.

The female applicant must be able to show she will not resort to public funds or work in the UK until she has full residence status. Previous visitor visas to the UK or an EU member state will count favorably. Previous visa refusals will count unfavorably.

The UK Home Office website is very informative and they do respond to enquiries and questions. After the fiancée visa is granted, she may enter the UK as many times as she likes during the visa duration, it allows multiple entries and will be six months in duration.

So how long does all this take? Usually it takes about forty-eight hours from the application submission appointment; her passport can be collected by a representative or sent back by courier. Americans and Australians who read the next section will be weeping if they read this first; they must wait up to a year!

After you are married in the UK, you then apply from within the UK to the Home Office for an FLR (Further Leave to Remain) visa; this will be a two year visa, following which you apply for an ILR (Indefinite Leave to Remain) visa, which as the name suggests, does not expire. About a year after that, she can apply for a UK passport if she wants one.

THE UNITED STATES OF AMERICA

In America the fiancée visa is called the K1. This is for when you plan to marry in America. If you marry abroad, the visa will be either a K3 or a CR1. The most common visa people apply for is the K1 fiancée visa. It is usually faster to get a K1 visa.

A K1 visa will be good for ninety days once your lady arrives, during which time you must be married or she must depart the US. To apply, you must be a US Citizen, both parties must be of a legal age to marry, both must be free to marry and you must have met personally within the past two years.

The petitioner (you) must have an income of at least 125 percent of the poverty level or assets sufficient to satisfy the US government. The amount of assets required varies depending on your income. It will be up to you to insure that you have sufficient income or assets.

The K1 process consists of several steps. Step one is assembling the K1 fiancée visa application and sending it to your regional service center along with the payment. Once you have mailed your application, the first thing you will receive is called an NOA-1 (Notice of Action 1) which will have a reference number. This means your application has been received; you can use this number to check on your case.

The next notification you receive is the NOA-2. This notice will take time. It means the regional center has approved your visa application and forwarded it to the NVC (National Visa Center). The NVC process usually goes fairly quickly. They do a name check for criminal records, domestic violence charges and similar. They assign your approval a case number and forward it to the appropriate embassy in the FSU.

Your fiancée will subsequently receive a packet with forms to fill out and instructions of what she needs to do to be ready for her personal interview. She will also need to obtain an appointment time for her interview. Prior to her interview, she will need to file the DS-230 Visa Application form, get a police report from every town she has lived in since the age of sixteen, in every name she has had (maiden and married). She will need more passport style photos, and she will need a medical exam at one of the approved clinics. She will also need some additional documentation and some information from you. This includes your financial data proving sufficient income or assets to support her, and if applicable, her child.

During this entire process, you are urged to assist your lady in every way possible. You will be dealing with the US Government and their requirements are very particular. The amount of documents you will be submitting is substantial and will likely be overwhelming to your lady. In order to avoid a rupture in your relationship, you should be prepared to be supportive emotionally and financially as she assembles and obtains English translations for her documents.

The final step in the visa process will be your lady's interview at the US embassy in her country. It is recommended that you try to accompany her to the interview, whether you are allowed to attend the actual interview or not is subject to local rules. (In Russia you can't, but most others you can.) However, at the very least, you will be demonstrating your commitment to her and your presence will be appreciated. In addition, within several days she is likely to have her visa and it would be a good thing if you are there with her when she first travels to America and clears customs. Her K1 visa is technically good for up to 180 days and then after her arrival in America, she has ninety days with which to marry or return to her country.

So how long does the K1 take? Usually it takes anywhere from six to nine months, occasionally up to a year. There are two service centers for the USCIS that process K1 applications, Vermont and California. Your filing will be based on the state in which you live.

The process is similar for a K3 visa. You and your lady will need to discuss in detail whether you wish to marry in her country or in America. Historically, K3 visas take a bit longer to process.

The third option is the CR1 visa, which is *significantly* different. The CR1 results in the immediate issuance of a green card and allows her to work, apply for a driver's license, travel, etc. In addition you will save about 50 percent of the costs of the filing fees since it will not be necessary for her to go through the Adjustment of Status process and the Removal of Conditions. The downside of a CR1 is that the approval time period is significantly greater than either a K1 or a K3.

After your marriage on either a K1 or a K3 visa and her successful relocation to America, you will be required to go through significant other filings with the US Government. This includes Adjustment of Status, Advanced Parole and numerous other steps ultimately leading to a green card and if she wishes, American citizenship. It is beyond the scope of this

Visas

book to delve into the entire process.

Please study the links contained on our resources website carefully. If you find the process overwhelming, do not hesitate to hire a professional service or a lawyer to assist you in the process.

AUSTRALIA

Getting into Australia is similar to the US in many respects. There are several visa options available. The fiancée visa is the preferred route for most. The fiancée visa is referred to as the "Prospective Marriage Visa" (Visa Subclass 300). The sponsor (you) must complete the appropriate forms and gather all available evidence of a genuine and ongoing relationship. You must include detailed documents substantiating your financial position, residency status and a host of other details.

You must then forward this data to your fiancée and she must complete all her documentation. She must have a formal police check completed from her current and any other country she has lived in during the preceding ten years. She must complete a medical check with an approved doctor in her country. Any documents in Russian must be translated, notarized and include the original copy in Russian also.

To start the application involves a simple phone call to the embassy in her country and making an appointment for an interview. The embassy will send her a questionnaire. This is a very simple form designed to insure that she has all documents ready and completed prior. An interview time will be set for her upon receipt by the embassy of the completed questionnaire.

The applicant arrives at the embassy in the morning and submits her

167

application. She is then required to return later in the day for the interview, leaving time for the officer to examine her documents. The interview will be quite intense for her; there will be a panel of two or three people and some in-depth and very personal questions. Next, the embassy will review the application and possibly request further information. This usually occurs within two weeks. So how long does all this take? Between ten months and a year is pretty normal.

After her visa is granted, she may enter Australia as many times as she likes during the visa duration; it allows multiple entries. She is also entitled to a tax number and she is free to work. You have nine months from her arrival to be married or she must leave the country. When you are married, an application must be submitted to change her visa to SC309 Temporary Spouse Visa.

CANADA

The Canadian Immigration and Citizenship authority is called the CIC. There is no such thing as a fiancée visa to Canada. You must marry her in another country, usually her own, before she will be permitted to immigrate.

Curiously, Canada does not have an income requirement to bring a spouse back except for the province of Quebec. The only time there would be an income requirement would be if you were in receipt of public funds. The principle seems to be they don't want to prevent you from being with your wife and they put up few obstacles in that regard. How refreshing!

There is only an interview if there are inconsistencies in the paperwork or if they suspect the marriage is not genuine. Other than that, she sends her papers to the embassy in her country of residence, while yours stay in Canada. Your paperwork is checked and then they tell you if you are approved to be a sponsor, it takes about a month for that decision.

However, the time factor comes into play in the FSU. The CIC claims there are usually a number of mistakes in women's paperwork such as missing or incorrect documents. So how long does all this take? Usually it takes somewhere in the region of six months to get the visa.

VISITOR VISAS

In an ideal world your lady would have visited you a few times and got a good feel for your country, and you would both have had the opportunity to visualize your future life together. For this you would need a visitor visa. For these purposes she is just a tourist. However, getting a visitor visa is not always easy, especially in America.

It is preferable for most visitor visa applicants to have a sponsor; that's you! Being a sponsor is little different to the fiancée visa process described above. The main difference with a visitor visa is the onus is on her to prove she has compelling reasons to go home and won't vanish into the ether forever the moment she arrives in your country.

She will present her case in a variety of ways, such as demonstrating she owns property, has a bank account with real money in it, has a decent job with a good salary, a child or elderly relative she must care for, etc. Prior foreign visas always help as they demonstrate that she has returned home before.

Whether she is given a tourist visa depends on the policy of the country where you are from. Predictably, the UK is quite straightforward and they claim only to reject 3 percent of applicants. Australia, Canada and mainland Europe make you jump through more hoops, but it is usually possible if the application looks credible.

As you would expect, the tourist visa situation for the US is *possible* but quite unlikely. Some men do manage to get women into the US on a tourist visa though. The US in fact even refused my wife a visa to travel with me, even though she had full UK residency rights, was married in the UK, and has a stepson and a business in the UK. The reason? Insufficient ties to the UK they said.

If my wife was refused with her word-perfect textbook application and glut of supporting documents, Sexy Sveta from Saratov stands less chance. Unfortunately, for most of you American guys, the first time she will see your country is when she arrives on a K1 or K3 visa.

MARRYING IN THE FSU

If you decide to marry in her country, you need to get certain documents together to be able to do this. They are mostly routine, but you must investigate what is required. The main document you need is a "certificate of no impediment" from your country which basically proves you are free and clear to marry. This will be issued usually by the courts or births and deaths registrar in your country. If you are divorced, you will need a certified copy of your divorce decree.

These documents usually need to be translated into Russian, Ukrainian, Estonian or whatever her local official language is. All documents and translations need to be notarized, apostilled or legalized according to the requirements of her country. Sometimes there is a waiting period to get these documents in your home country, as the request must sometimes be advertised somewhere for a set limit of time, usually twenty-one days.

Most of the FSU has a rule where the foreigner must be in their country for a set period of time, usually thirty days, before being allowed to marry. As with many things, this can be reduced in *exceptional* circumstances. Those circumstances will usually be created and recorded by the person who you bribe in the ZAGS office who has the correct rubber stamp to authorize it. Thankfully, your fiancée will deal with all that for you; you must only lurk in the background having given her some cash while the furtive deed is done.

ZAGS (called RAGS in Ukraine) is the civil registry office. This office knows everything from birthdates to deaths, divorces, the date you got your university diploma, your driver's license information, etc. They keep records of when your children were born and where. They even know when Uncle Sasha was released from prison. ZAGS are most famous for weddings. It's where you get a wedding permit and where your civil (legal) wedding will take place. By international treaty, a marriage in Russia is legal in every western country. So is a divorce.

Many Russian ladies want a church wedding also, but a church wedding in Russia or Ukraine is not a legal wedding unlike many other parts of the world. To complicate matters further, many Russian women believe that while a civil state wedding is the legal one, it has no validity in the eyes of God. So like most Russian/Ukrainian couples you may be enjoying not one, but two ceremonies for your wife to feel as if you are married for real. One for the state and one for God. An in-depth look at the whole ZAGS/RAGS process can be found on our resources website detailed at the back of the book.

Now you must apply for her visa for your country which can occur as quickly as twenty-four hours for the UK and up to a year for the US.

So eventually the day arrives when she is coming to live with you in your country. You have traveled a long way in your endeavor and it's about to come to fruition. At last you can relax, can't you? Sorry, but no. This is where the hardest and quite possibly the most expensive of your journey begins.

Chapter Fourteen
After Her Arrival — Helping Her Adapt and Creating a Family

Congratulations! She is now ready to arrive in her new country. Your home is now hers. She will quickly be making changes!

As a side note, before she arrives you *must* make sure your home is impeccably clean. The clutter must be removed, the floors and furniture must be cleaned, and everything should be spotless. Visualize for a moment that you are planning on selling your home and you want it to look its best for a prospective buyer. If need be, hire professionals to help you with your cleaning. The same level of preparation should be extended to your yard or garden and even your car.

By all means buy a new mattress and box springs (divan base). She will appreciate knowing that she is the first and only one to have joined you on your new mattress. Do not underestimate the importance of this one issue. You would be well-advised to discuss this matter with her prior to her arrival; she may even prefer that you wait and allow her to make the choice of a new bed.

Explain to her that you know your home is not ideal and that you need her help in making it the perfect home for the both of you. She will need something to focus on when she gets there and will have fun changing everything. It will solidify the idea that it is now her home also. The yard and garden are not safe either; expect within a few months an explosion of color and flowers where before had been beer tins and apathy.

Realize that you will be doing the heavy work in the garden and most likely maintaining her creative efforts thereafter.

After she has finished on the curtains, bedding, furniture and things you didn't even think about, she will probably be upgrading your wardrobe. After all, she now has only a few months to make you respectable looking husband material if you are marrying in your country.

Assuming you are marrying in your country, the two of you will also be planning for your wedding. Remember that you will be paying for the wedding and remember to provide her with guidance and emotional support. The two of you should discuss what kind of wedding you want and you should plan on helping her make it happen. The father of the bride will most likely not be helping you. He cannot afford to contribute and even if he can, with the economic disparity that exists between you and her father, it may look bad if you accept traditional help in this regard.

Smaller weddings are usually chosen as her lack of guests and your many will swamp her if you invite three hundred people you know. Again, in the US her family is most unlikely to be able to attend due to the visa situation, but inviting her parents may be worth a shot if you can afford to pay for their travel and hotel. In the UK, Europe and elsewhere it is more likely to be able to get her family visitor visas, as their daughter's wedding is a superb reason to request a visa. If you do invite her family, offer them their tickets and accommodation as a gift from both of you. If her family does have an opportunity for a visit in these circumstances, they will feel so much better having seen the environment where she will live. This will pay you dividends as they will encourage and support her later on when she feels homesick, which she will.

After Her Arrival

So it's the wedding day! Everyone has his or her own ideas about how it should be done and if a civil or a church wedding is preferable. You will find the route that suits you both through conversation with her. Make sure she has some female assistance. If her family is not present, you maybe can find her some women, maybe from your family, or maybe she has made a friend already who will help her. Depending on her English level, make certain you practice her spoken part of the ceremony again and again with her until she is word perfect. She will be nervous enough on the day anyway; in front of wedding guests is not the time to have her language flunk out. You might even consider doing part of the ceremony together in Russian.

Have you considered a honeymoon? Some couples don't bother due to visa difficulties; some take a later one. Traveling outside of your country at this early stage may cause issues with her visa. Maybe you can take a honeymoon in your country? Men from countries other than America sometimes consider a foreign honeymoon to places where a visa is not required. Depending on the political climate, this may include some of the Caribbean countries, Israel, Egypt, Thailand and Turkey. It will be up to the two of you to determine where you want to go and if there are any visa issues.

Now that you are happily married, do you feel that you are at the end of your road? Mission accomplished! Now *at last* you can relax can't you? Er...... not quite yet, dear reader!

Now you have to deal with all the mundane day-to-day things she needs. She will probably need English classes; you need to arrange this. She may want to continue her education. She may want to find a job. She will need a social security card (or a national insurance number elsewhere). If in America she will need medical insurance. You should introduce her to your doctor, set up a bank account for her and make sure she has good access from your (or her new) computer to the internet and the ability to phone home regularly.

As the new husband of a Russian lady, you should plan on taking as much time off from your work as humanly possible to help her adapt. The importance of this cannot be underestimated. If she is stranded alone in your home, severe boredom and homesickness can quickly kick in. Remember in all likelihood she was extremely active and busy in her home country.

She will almost certainly need to drive and at this point you find out that her Russian license (if she has one) is not exchangeable although it may have a limited time validity depending on your country. Driving will be an excellent self-esteem builder for her and you should get her driving as soon as possible. In the long-term, a (non-EU) FSU driver's license has all the value of yesterday's bus ticket, so she will need to get a local one. This means her English being at a level to take instruction and take her driver's test. However, if she can drive already and has a Russian license, the basic rules for some countries are below.

THE UNITED KINGDOM: A Russian driver's license is valid as a full license in the UK, but only for up to one year from the point she becomes resident, after which she must have a UK license to continue driving. They are not exchangeable, so that means she should take her driving test within the first year.

With the visitor, fiancée and FLR visa system, the actual date she becomes resident is open to interpretation. Whether it is from when she arrives on a fiancée visa, when she was married, when her first post-marital residence visa started is a little unclear. Nobody seems to check.

The right to residence and actually being physically resident are quite different. If one flits in and out of the UK, one could legitimately claim to be here visiting but not yet resident as such prior to the last entry, for example, "Oh yes, I was entitled to be resident from last year but I actually was resident from when I arrived last month." Based on this, some people stretch a Russian license's validity out for as much two years in the UK with a country-hopping oft-traveling woman.

AUSTRALIA: In Australia a Russian/Ukrainian driver's license is valid for three months before she must take her driving test. Some Aussie's report there is a way around it. In Australia you may drive on an International Driving Permit (basically a translation of your foreign license) until you are a permanent resident or citizen.

THE UNITED STATES: In the US the rules differ depending on your state. New York recognizes any license from anywhere in the world, but in Florida a Russian/Ukrainian license is completely worthless. You need either an EAD (work permit) or a green card to get a license. It's only valid as long as your immigration paperwork is, plus you must take four hours of drug and alcohol classes and a written test followed by a practical driving test. In Massachusetts, a Russian or FSU license is valid for a year only, similar to the UK rules. Those three example states are so different and represent such disparity in the States; you American guys need to check the situation in your state.

CANADA: Visitors (six months or less) are fine with a valid license issued in their country of residency if accompanied by a passport or International Driver's Permit issued in country of residency. You have ninety days to switch to a local license in the province of your residency if you are a visa holder or claim residency in Canada. A valid license from former country of residency, written general knowledge exam and road test will be required. In provinces with graduated licensing programs, the applicant must hold a current driver's license in their former country of residency for more than two years or will end up with the equivalent provisional license (a license with learner/novice restrictions) and have to graduate the program as anyone else would. Should an applicant fail a road test, his or her license will be confiscated until such time as they pass (this means unable to drive at all). Failure of the written exam means a re-test but not loss of license. International Driver's Permits alone are not valid.

Now you have finished yawning about driver's license rules, we move on to what happens when real life kicks in and her real adaptation to her new country starts. As soon as she arrives, expect little sense out of her. She will want to sleep, sleep and sleep some more. This may last a few days. You will notice over the coming months she may sleep inordinately long periods of time. I have a friend who calls this phenomenon "sleepy girl syndrome." Let her ease into her new country slowly; do not overwhelm her with activities and people. She will spend the first few weeks poking around the house, making her spaces, installing her stuff, learning about your appliances and things like that.

Ease her in nice and gently; take her to restaurants for the first few days in the evenings while she gets a feel for the neighborhood and the people. Keep the pressure off her. Go to the supermarket with her and keep in mind that she will want to poke around herself and may take awhile reading labels while she works out what different things are amidst the unfamiliar packaging she will encounter. If she feels confident, let her have some time by herself in the supermarket moving at her own speed. Encouraging independence is what you are aiming at early on. To do this she must have a basic familiarity with the immediate area and know where places are, so a guided tour is advised in the first few days.

Show her where the hairdressers and the local salons are and any other places you think may interest her. Make sure she has plenty of cash in her pocket for anything she needs when you are out (not credit cards until she is familiar with them). This is where the subtle pressure to learn English in the previous months begins to reap dividends; if she is mute she can't even go and get her nails or hair done without your explaining to the salon woman what she wants. She will find this degrading. Encourage her to try to speak to people; she may be shy at first, not confident with her language, but with a little perseverance her confidence will grow exponentially in a matter of weeks. Make sure she has a mobile phone from day one with plenty of minutes or credit on it and all your numbers programmed in. That way she has the ability to call you if she has any difficulties.

If she has a young child, early provision must be made to get the child into school. If the child has zero or little English, there are often special classes or government programs that will assist in that regard. This differs very much from country to country. You *must* help her and her child obtain English skills as quickly and efficiently as possible.

Before she arrives, speak to your local education department to see what the arrangements are for immigrant children in your area. If the child is attending a local school, you will need to show your new wife how the child gets to and from school. Again, this is gently forcing independence and confidence at a very early stage.

The first few weeks and maybe months while she is getting comfortable and everything is new and exciting is a fun time. This is the honeymoon period if you like, and as with any relationship the honeymoon period does not last that long. After this is when you need to be alert to the homesickness kicking in; it can come any time up to maybe a year, but it definitely will come.

Everyone is different and no two women will have the same feelings. It can be as minor as her just having bouts of depression thinking of her family and homeland that she snaps out of with logical thought. However, it can be more extreme and many women decide they don't like their new country, the food, the air, the water, the lack of snow and all kinds of things will be singled out as terrible and different from home. One man I know was at his wit's end when his wife proclaimed the sky was even different and not as nice as the one she used to see in Ukraine!

She may have a period here where she doubts herself and her entire relocation decision; it will be a very real and awful experience for her. All you can do is comfort her and be exceptionally supportive. You can assure her that it is a perfectly normal phase she is going through that all women in her position go through. Do your best to convince her it will pass. It almost always *will* pass in a few months when she has found things to do and she feels much more familiar with her new home and country.

After Her Arrival

One woman who was asked about this said, "When I look back at my first months in England, I cried all the time for the first month. It took me about a year to stop complaining. Luckily, my husband was very patient and understanding."

Many women, especially those who have not traveled much, imagine life in the West to be very easy. We are all *rich* of course and often little is known about the true realities of life or where the money comes from. The realization that we must work sometimes seven days a week and are burdened with humdrum things like mortgages, loans, alimony, child support and other responsibilities can be overlooked. Real life can hit some women quite hard if they are unprepared for it. What looks like a rich Western lifestyle to a Russian may seem hollow when she discovers your expensive car is financed and you don't actually own that lovely house. The bank does for the next twenty years.

Her adaptation is not only to you and your life, but also to your culture. Remember, in Russia if you have a big house and nice car you probably own them outright and paid cash for them. It will mystify her why anyone would use a credit card to buy groceries. "Are we actually so poor that we need credit to eat?" she will wonder. One woman we know told her friends back home that life in the West is an illusion, all paid for with other peoples' money and nobody seems to actually own anything. If you think about it, was she wrong?

Something else that may hinder her adaptation is financial worry about her parents or family back in Russia. Her salary may have been an important contribution to the family finances when she lived there. Now she has moved abroad, her parents (especially if elderly), may suffer as a result. You need to address this matter and alleviate it before it happens.

When you marry a Russian woman, you also marry her family. Her family is now your family. In Russian society, the offspring look after their older family members and they take that responsibility seriously.

Leaving behind parents, especially elderly ones, is no easy task for a woman. She will feel guilty for doing this and will be balancing that guilt with her desire to have her own husband and happy family. All you can do in this situation is throw some money at the problem.

It may only be $250 a month that makes all the difference to her remaining family and that should be hardly noticeable to you. If they are happy, she will be happy, and she will feel less guilty about *abandoning* them. Many women expect to send some monthly financial support back to the family; certainly in the first year or two this will mean you will be funding this.

It would be wise to discuss this topic tactfully and in depth with her before she relocates. It may also be the case that she wants to make their life easier in some ways before she relocates. Something as simple as a washing machine or a new refrigerator for them may make her feel better about leaving.

Situations differ and families differ. If she has brothers and sisters, it may not be necessary or expected that you contribute. If she has left behind a lone elderly parent, you could be funding medical necessities and outside care (if available) at some stage, not to mention paying for more frequent flights back to visit. Many men don't need to send any money yet others fund the entire household expenses. Inquiries should also be made about a neighbor or family friend to keep an eye on an elderly lone parent

After Her Arrival

in case of need and payment to that person needs to be addressed as well. This is an often-overlooked post-relocation expense.

Adaptation is multi-faceted; it can be the smallest things that a woman likes that helps her adapt and feel happy in her new country. Making sure she is in touch with her friends and family as often as she wants, and that she is assured of her loved ones welfare, can only reap dividends in your marriage.

My wife was asked on one of the forums she occasionally participates in, "What things were difficult for you to adapt to? What was easy?" Her reply was so informative that I will reproduce it here:

> There are several types of adaptation: Physical, social and psychological.
>
> Physical: My only physical adaptation problem was food. I can't eat several types of food, for example Indian food that is popular here. The bread and meat are different. However, I can find things I do like; we have many Russian food shops and also I like the good quality organic food and the seafood. The tea is excellent quality.
>
> Social: I don't miss my friends in Russia; I can still speak with them whenever I want on the telephone. I have Russian friends here from my hometown. However, my husband is my best friend. I very often interact with local men and women; I go to the gym, for beauty treatments, etc. I find the local people are friendly; they always have many questions about Russia, my adaptation and my view of England. I have a very close relationship with my parents. They have visited me in England. Of course my Mother misses me, but we speak several times a week on the phone, and being in England, I am only seven hours door-to-door, so visits are possible without it being a military operation.

Psychological adaptation: I always felt I would live abroad since I was a teenager. I traveled as a tourist all over Europe; Europe was not unfamiliar for me. The country was not important for me; more important was the man. Fortunately, I am very lucky; I found my man and his country now is my country. My optimistic view helped me very much with my adaptation, as I am an optimist by nature. My knowledge and education as a psychologist has helped me very much with my adaptation also.

Almost without exception, Russian women have had the negative feelings phase in varying degrees after they relocate. It almost always passes. The important thing is to make sure she is not bored; a busy mind has less time to fret about such things. A patient and understanding husband is only part of what gets a woman through the adaptation to life abroad. Much also depends on the determination of the woman herself.

In the coming months, she will disparage many aspects of your culture and life in your country. Negative comparisons will be drawn between her country and yours. Naturally, it will all be your fault because you took her away from her homeland. Everything will be different; nothing will be the same. She will miss her parents terribly. Did I mention it will all be your fault? This is a storm you must ride out with as much patience as you can find within yourself. It will most likely pass, although when you are in the thick of it you will sometimes have doubts about that.

If you are at work all day, leaving her vegetating at home with daytime TV will make her feel even more isolated and depressed. In this situation, she may need a job, any job, even a volunteer job at a local school or charity. Anything that gets her out of the house and doing something, meeting people, talking to people, looking around. etc., will

After Her Arrival

help. If she is just sitting at home, all the communication avenues you have opened up for her will just make her spend all day on the computer or phone to Russia; that will be counter-productive for you both.

Be prepared for some minor lifestyle changes and more especially a few things that we accept as standard practice in the home, for logical reasons, will not be so when you are married to a Russian. There are a few typical traits that many married men recount, the first of which is that you will be sweltering at home in 90+ degree heat much of the time. (Remember those hot Russian apartments?) The items she thinks should live in the refrigerator will also surprise you. A cooked chicken may sit on the kitchen work surface for three days uncovered; she will insist vehemently this is not detrimental to health.

Similarly, orange juice, white wine and other things traditionally kept in the refrigerator will languish in a warm cupboard. So what does go in the refrigerator? Well to a Russian, vegetables, cosmetics and bread live quite naturally there. You will encounter many unusual domestic habits; trying to convince her otherwise will be difficult. Better to let your orange juice stay in the fridge and let hers to ferment quietly in a warm cupboard.

Another thing you need to have an eye out for is the post-immigration weight factor. Most new arrivals tend to start putting on some weight a few months after their arrival. This is caused by a combination of things. Daytime boredom is the main culprit; a tasty snack or four goes well with that daytime TV mentioned above. A fridge stuffed to the gills with high fat snacks does not help and neither does her new sedentary lifestyle.

The woman that you married now enjoys a higher standard of living in material terms than would have been likely had she stayed in her country. She probably isn't going out to work each day to make the money to just get by like she did before. She will be enjoying her new lifestyle spending her time "making cozy home" for you.

Her lifestyle is now very different compared to what she had been used to. Now she isn't walking to work; she isn't carrying groceries from the bus stop up many flights of stairs any more. There are several ways of approaching this little problem, but approach it you must, lest your shiny new slim wife becomes in less than two years, bigger than the local women you went to Russia to avoid. (If you doubt this, look at her mother, is she slim? Russian Babushka's seldom are.) One favored technique is to renew her wardrobe shortly after her arrival with plenty of nice expensive stuff if you have any money left. This has the twofold effect of making her look even lovelier and when some of this nice new stuff begins to feel a little tight, she will immediately notice herself without a word from you and take immediate steps in silence.

Another step you should have planned early on to help with her integration and adaptation is to get her a membership in your local gym. The exercise factor will do her figure no harm and will help to counteract the change of lifestyle described above. It probably will improve your figure too, as she will quickly decide that you need a workout with her.

This will do you no harm and it may help her, as it will take her a while to be confident enough to rebuff the approaches of the local hopeful men in the gym on her own. There is nothing quite like a lycra clad Russian woman with a foxy accent stretching and bouncing in a gym; it is guaranteed to have the local men drooling around her like the proverbial

After Her Arrival

flies around honey.

Beautiful slim women are quite abundant in the FSU; in the West they are less common and thus attract more attention. It will take her time to adjust to men leering, whistling, tooting car horns or whatever they do in your locale when a sexy woman is sighted. Remember in her society, most women are quite slim; long hair, short skirts and high heels are the norm. In the West, a typical Russian look can quite literally stop traffic. Help her to laugh at these things and remind her that you have not overlooked your good fortune. Handled well, she will enjoy the attention and soon feel confident and sexy in her new country.

It is a temptation for many men to try to hook up their new wife with other Russian-speaking people they can find in their locality. If you feel compelled to do this, realize it may not be your best day's work. Not everyone will have been as diligent as you in his search for a Russian woman and there is no saying the type of character she may encounter. Her new pal may just want to go out night clubbing every night without the husbands. She may be a green card girl, a woman with loose morals or an inappropriate role model in other ways. Your wife will find a few Russian speakers over time on her own; it's surprising where they pop up and they seem to have inbuilt radar to detect each other.

If you were introduced to a random man from your country while living abroad, how much would you likely have in common with him apart from speaking the same language? Are you likely to become best friends with a random man in the street? It is possible, but generally unlikely. It is the same thing; the only thing your wife will have in common with other Russian speakers is the fact that they happen to live in the same country and speak the same language. That is not a sound basis for a friendship. She may feel such introductions are contrived and avoid such situations in any event. Many men imagine they are doing their wife a great favor in this regard; usually they are not.

If your town has a Russian Orthodox Church, and only if she expresses a desire to go, you should take her there. She will meet Russian speakers there and being Christians, one would hope that they are decent folk. She may form a few natural friendships with people in the church group, but again, don't push that; leave it to nature.

I have heard of instances in the Orthodox churches where women have been ignored completely. This has been because some of these Russian immigrants arrived in your country the hard way, under their own steam and worked very hard to do so. Women who have married local men are sometimes frowned upon because they took the *easy route* and arrived to what is perceived by the others as instant riches.

Similarly, do not push her into friendships with your local women thinking you are doing her a favor either. Many of your local women will be jealous of the slim foreign woman; she is from the breed that "comes over here and steals all our men" that they read about in the media. Remember that your local women have the traits you went to Russia to avoid; do you want to teach her to be a *Western woman?*

Just let her meet people naturally; don't be surprised if it takes her a year or more to make a friend. There is no rush; she may not need the company of others so much while she settles in to her new country.

You must be observant and cautious about any new friends however. You as a local, can tell a whole lot about local people in an instant; per-

After Her Arrival

haps certain behavior, maybe an accent, or other subtle cultural things that a Russian wouldn't see. If she befriends someone who is patently unsuitable, it is your responsibility to guide and advise her, without being dictatorial, in the right direction.

Remember, you have done your homework on Russia, the culture and its people already; others you know will be quite ignorant about what you both have done and your respective motivations. Your friends and associates may grill her with nonsensical questions about Putin, Medvedev, Russia, mail-order brides, "how do you like it here?" and other such trivia. Keep an eye out in social situations for these things and help her out if she gets buttonholed this way which can easily happen.

If you investigate a little, you should find a Russian food shop in your area or reasonably nearby. If not, you will find a Ukrainian or maybe a Polish shop. In the UK, one can now find a *Polski Sklep* (Polish Shop) in most towns. Although they are not Russian, the language is not dissimilar and many older Poles can speak Russian. More to the point, the food is almost the same. She can find familiar things like her Smetana, Kefir, Pelmeni, Seledka and Gretchka in a Polish shop too. If a true Russian shop, they will have some Russian DVD's and newspapers which also will be nice for her.

You can make your computer Russian friendly quite easily. A Russian/English keyboard can be had from many places online, even eBay. (As can Cyrillic keyboard stickers.) Set your computer up for Russian language by going to your Control Panel, click on "Settings," and then double click on "Regional and Language Options," "Languages" then "Details." If you then click "Add," from the drop down menu that you see, find Russian, and then click "OK." You should be able to type using Cyrillic now, either by pressing left Alt + Shift, or by clicking on the language icon on your tool bar. (The icon should appear as "EN" if you are typing in English or "RU" if you are typing in Russian/Cyrillic) Ukrainian can be similarly added.

It is easy to go too far with sourcing Russian things for her; there comes a point when it will start to make her homesick. Many men make the mistake of subscribing to Russian TV channels, newspapers and magazines and any Russian language media they can obtain. They seem to recreate a mini-Russia in their house. That is going too far. It does not help her to learn English; it does not help adaptation and it will not offer anything beneficial to your marriage. She has her friends and parents at the end of the phone, radio streams in Russian are available free on the internet, together with the odd Russian newspaper and DVD mentioned above and some familiar foodstuffs. That is enough. Moscow Channel One television by satellite is unnecessary.

During the early months after her arrival, the topic of a return visit to her homeland should be discussed. It will be on her mind and a tiny part of her fears will be that she will never see her homeland ever again. Plan together a month when either she or both of you will visit. Do not make it too soon, however. Make sure she has time to adapt to your country first.

If she visits her homeland while she is still in the depression stage of the adaptation process, it will look so much better than it did. It is familiar and it will suddenly feel like home again. Several men have let their wives visit Russia too soon after relocation and had great difficulty convincing

After Her Arrival

them they should come back home afterwards.

Visiting together is not a bad idea, but you may get bored if you are there too long as she will want to visit all her family and friends and tell them all about her new life. Also, if you live a very long flight away, it may not be reasonable to go for just a week or ten days. She may want two or three weeks or maybe even a month every year.

For instance, my wife goes annually for three weeks; I join her to visit our family and do things with her for the last week or ten days of that visit. That way she can do all her family and friends stuff before I arrive, and we can enjoy Russia together like a small holiday the rest of the time.

Assuming she has enough English when she arrives to get by, you can expect it to take between one and two years before she is reasonably well-adapted and integrated. It will likely take this long for her to get her driver's license, fluent English language and to get past her adaptation issues. There will never be one particular day when you can say her adaptation is complete, but there will come a time when your *Russian wife* becomes *your wife who happens to be Russian*. The distinction is subtle but when you pass it you will understand what I mean and you will recognize it, and only then will you know most of the hard work is behind you.

Future financial planning is something that absolutely must be considered. You should insure that you have an adequate estate plan in place in the event of your untimely demise. You owe it to your wife to make sure she understands what documents exist and what happens in the event something happens to you. This is especially critical since so many of our estate planning documents are totally without parallel in the FSU countries.

I would caution that the laws in each country (and in the US, each state) are different. Nonetheless, each of you needs a comprehensive estate plan. This begins with a will. In the event of a more sizable estate the will is frequently accompanied by a trust agreement. And, of course, there are durable powers of attorney and living wills to consider. You will need to work with a competent estate planning lawyer.

Those among you who have children from prior marriages must be cognizant as to how you wish to divide your largesse. Those who are business owners must also pay attention to succession plans for the business. Life insurance is another consideration. Do you have adequate insurance? Who are the beneficiaries?

After formulating a comprehensive plan and executing the appropriate documents, the next logical step involves explaining how everything is set up to your wife. She may or may not be qualified (either legally or in actuality) to act as your personal representative or executor. If not, a close relative, friend or advisor must be included in the process. Certainly, at a minimum, a thorough explanation of the documents together with copies of the documents and instructions as to who to call and what to do should be provided to your wife. You may wish to consider having some of this information translated into Russian for her.

Your explanation must also include instructions relative to any liabilities which may exist, e.g. mortgages, etc., and should also include your thoughts on the disposition of assets and personal property, as well as services and burial.

Please remember that these ladies who we so blithely import are human beings who deserve our utmost respect for the sacrifices they make for us and the new world into which they have come for us. We owe them nothing less than a full disclosure and a level of security so as to allow them to continue their lives in a reasonable manner in our absence.

We are almost at the end of the book. I sincerely hope you have benefited and learned from what has been written. I have tried to be as comprehensive as possible within the limited constraints of a single book and have tried to describe the process to you without the rose-colored glasses that some people seem to see Russian women through.

It is not always a bed of roses being the husband of a Russian woman. When I personally embarked upon this journey I had no idea what I was in for. I wish someone had told me in advance. Some of it was very hard work as we did it the hard way, without advice and shortcuts such as you have just read. It is not easy or cheap to find a Russian wife as you have learned, but be patient and you will find yourself a princess and it will indeed all have been worth it. It is our wish that all of you find the journey as rewarding as we have.

Chapter Fifteen
Other Resources

We have come a long way since the pre World Wide Web days when the only way to find a Russian woman was to see them in grainy black and white photos in subscription magazines and contact them through snail mail. Now with the whole internet at our fingertips and Google to do the searching, life is much easier.

There are thousands upon thousands of supposed resources on Russian women out there. Unfortunately, not all of them present accurate information. Many sites that masquerade as genuine information resources are fronts for unscrupulous agencies and others hoping to make a fast buck, giving you nothing substantive in exchange.

One can find any number of *e-books* on the internet about Russian women written by agency shills and the ill-informed that are hopelessly out of date. Anyone can write an e-book, put it out there, and hope to empty your pocket of a few Pounds, Euros, or Dollars. Likewise, anyone can put up a website and say almost anything they want on it. Sorting the wheat from the chaff on the internet is always a hard task with a subject such as this. The sites that get high on Google are usually the ones with the biggest advertising budgets, which does not necessarily equate to those with the most up-to-date or accurate content. Nor are they always the most trustworthy.

On the other hand, internet forums about Russian women are often a useful resource. An internet forum is a website for holding discussions and posting user-generated content. Internet forums are also known as message boards, discussion boards or bulletin boards. A sense of virtual community often develops around forums that have many regular users, many have active social scenes, live chat rooms, and other things going on that add to the camaraderie one can enjoy there. Forums are particularly useful for reading reports of scammers, scam agencies, locating service providers, cheap travel or brushing up on aspects of fast changing immigration rules pertaining to your particular situation and country.

Many people prefer to just read and not participate, while at the other end of the spectrum, some people can become annoying self-proclaimed experts on everything. There are always a few service providers and agency owners snooping around hoping to snare new clients, some of whom do so by covert shilling via the private message systems with multiple identities rather than adopting an honest approach. Some people cross-inhabit all the forums, not always under the same name and some of these people seem to have grudges with each other from days gone by and disbanded or abandoned forums of yore.

Nonetheless, the forums are useful. Do not get sucked into the political shenanigans and character assassinations that go on; be relaxed with the cyber bullies and know-it-all cantankerous old men sporting trophy wives, of which most forums have one or two. Get involved and have fun by all means, but do not take it all too seriously.

There are several forums relevant to the topic of finding a Russian bride, the better ones I am aware of are below. There will be others of course but I do not know them all.

Russian-women-related conversation forums

Ruadventures.com – Known as RUA. I have been an active administrator and moderator on this forum since its inception, and during the writing of this book was given the opportunity to purchase it (which my wife and I did) as the former owners had lost interest. We have expert administrators, moderators and advisors from the US, Australia, Canada and the UK.

RUA was started to create a place devoid of the bickering, trolling and spamming that occurs on other Russian women related forums. It is friendly and welcoming to the newbie, is very well moderated and has a wealth of highly experienced contributors from all over the world (many Russian ladies too) eager to help - and all completely free of charge.

Russiandetective.forumup.org – A forum run by russian-detective.com where one can post scammer information for the benefit of others. Not terribly active, but a good resource that seems well moderated.

Waytorussia.net – A selection of services are offered on this site such as flights, trains, visas and accommodations. Not always the cheapest of course but well regarded by many. There is a small conversation forum there also, but it is not very active. The site also has some cultural and practical information.

Visajourney.com – An American immigration visa information site with much useful data, forms, instructions, contact information and active forums that seem to be able to answer very complex questions about the US visa situations one may encounter.

Redtape.ru – A conversation forum primarily for ex-pats living in

Other Resources

Russia containing some useful information on there for the traveler.

Online Translators

Translate.ru – Online text and website translator, probably the best one but slow.

Google.com/translate_t – As above. Good quality, free and fast.

Babelfish.altavista.com – Not as good as Google.

Our internet resource site to accompany this book

We have created a small website at **www.RussianWomenBook.co.uk** as a further resource to support this book. On there you will find all the information above and much more besides. All you need to do is click on the individual links. As the world of Russian dating is a constantly changing place, resources can and do change. An agency that is believed to be popular and honest today may not be tomorrow.

On these web pages, we try to give you honest and up-to-date informational links, some of it linking back into specific topics on our RUA conversation forums, most linking to elsewhere. We have no bias in this regard; we do not particularly seek to channel you to our "friends" or our own services. Indeed the reason we acquired the RUA conversation forums is so that men could get honest unbiased advice from others who have used different processes, agencies and resources. We prefer you to make an informed choice about the service providers and resources you use.

It is our intent that you will go into this adventure as well informed as possible and having all available information at your fingertips. We hope to see you on the **RUAdventures.com** conversation forums!

www.ingramcontent.com/pod-product-compliance
Lightning Source LLC
Chambersburg PA
CBHW020759160426
43192CB00006B/376